Ted's Only Hope

"You're a great rider, Lucy!" Elizabeth said encouragingly. "You'd have a real chance of winning the prize money!"

Lucy looked from Elizabeth to Ted and back again. "I can't," Lucy said, her voice nearly cracking. "I'd like to help you keep Thunder, Ted, but there's no way I could do what you're asking."

"Do what?" Ellen asked, riding up on Snow White.

"We're trying to talk Lucy into competing on Thunder in my place," Ted explained.

"But I can't," Lucy repeated sadly.

"You mean you won't," Ellen taunted. "I knew you were all talk, Lucy Benson! It's easy to show off when there's no pressure. But you're afraid you'd fail in a real competition, aren't you?"

Lucy stuck out her chin. "That's not it at all, Ellen!"

"It doesn't matter," Elizabeth told Lucy in a soothing voice. "We understand." But Elizabeth wasn't quite sure she did understand. Couldn't Lucy see that she was Ted's only hope?

D1381640

The SWEET VALLEY TWINS series, published by Bantam Books. Ask your bookseller for any titles you have missed.

SWEET VALLEY TWINS SUPER CHILLERS

SWEET VALLEY TWINS SUPER EDITIONS

SWEET VALLEY TWINS

Lucy Takes the Reins

Written by
Jamie Suzanne

Created by
FRANCINE PASCAL

BANTAM BOOKS
NEW YORK · TORONTO · LONDON · SYDNEY · AUCKLAND

LUCY TAKES THE REINS

A BANTAM BOOK 0 553 40189 0

Originally published in U.S.A. by Bantam Skylark Books

First publication in Great Britain

PRINTING HISTORY
Bantam edition published 1991
Sweet Valley High ® and Sweet Valley Twins are registered
trademarks of Francine Pascal.

Conceived by Francine Pascal.

Produced by Daniel Weiss Associates, Inc., 33 West 17th Street,
New York, NY 10011

Cover art by James Mathewuse.

Bantam Books are published by Transworld Publishers Ltd.,
61–63 Uxbridge Road, Ealing, London W5 5SA,
in Australia by Transworld Publishers (Australia) Pty. Ltd.,
15–23 Helles Avenue, Moorebank, NSW 2170, and in New
Zealand by Transworld Publishers (N.Z.) Ltd., Cnr. Moselle
and Waipareira Avenues, Henderson, Auckland.

Made and printed in Great Britain by
BPCC Hazell Books
Aylesbury, Bucks, England
Member of BPCC Ltd.

Lucy
Takes the
Reins

One

"I may never move again!" Jessica Wakefield groaned. She lay back on the picnic blanket and closed her eyes.

"How many hot dogs did you eat, anyway?" asked her twin sister, Elizabeth, as she helped Mrs. Wakefield pack the family's leftover food.

"Three," Jessica mumbled.

"*Three* hot dogs?"

"Well, I was hungry," Jessica said defensively. "I worked up an appetite swimming."

"The next time we come to Secca Lake for a picnic, I'll have to remember to pack more food," Mrs. Wakefield said with a smile as she closed the lid on the cooler.

"Come on, Jess." Elizabeth stood up and extended her hand. "I know just the thing to help you work off all those calories!"

Jessica opened one eye. "A nap?"

"No, a walk! There's a riding trail that winds around the lake and through the woods. I thought if we followed it we might see some horses."

Jessica closed her eye again. "Wake me up when you get back, Lizzie."

Elizabeth grabbed her sister's hand and yanked her up. "Come on, Jess," she urged. "It'll be fun!"

"Oh, all right." Jessica yawned and stretched her arms over her head. "But I don't see what the big deal is about seeing some giant, smelly animals. If horses had any brains, they wouldn't let people sit on their backs and boss them around!"

Elizabeth shook her head. There was no point in trying to explain to Jessica the excitement of horses and riding. But she knew what her sister did find exciting. "Maybe we'll see a cute *boy* riding a giant, smelly horse," she suggested with a wry smile.

Jessica brightened. "Well, come on, then! What are we waiting for?"

Sometimes it's hard to believe we're identical twins, Elizabeth thought to herself as she and her sister walked toward the big grove of trees that skirted one side of the lake. Just like Elizabeth, Jessica had silky, sun-streaked blond hair and sparkling blue-green eyes. In fact, everything about them was the same, right down to the tiny dimples in their left cheeks.

But their personalities made it easy to tell the twins apart. Elizabeth was the older twin by four minutes, although it sometimes seemed more like four years. She was trustworthy and sensible, and loved school. Much of her free time was spent working on *The Sweet Valley Sixers*, the sixth-grade newspaper that she had helped to found. Her dedication spilled over into her friendships, as well. She loved having long, heart-to-heart conversations with her closest friends, and there was nothing that made her happier than spending time curled up with a good book.

For her part, Jessica couldn't understand why Elizabeth would *ever* want to be alone with a book when she could be having fun with a big group of friends. Jessica belonged to the Unicorns, an exclusive group of the most popular and snobbiest girls at Sweet Valley Middle School. When she wasn't spending time with the Unicorns, Jessica was usually on the phone with one of them, exchanging the latest gossip about clothes and boys.

"There's the riding trail up ahead," Jessica said, pointing through the trees. "But I don't see any horses—*or* any cute boys!"

"Let's wait a few minutes," Elizabeth said as she sat down on a layer of soft pine needles at the base of a large pine just off the trail. "It seems like ages since I've been to the stable," she said wistfully. "I've been so busy with homework and the *Sixers* lately."

"You ought to stop by for a visit," Jessica suggested. "Remember, there's the jumping competition coming up. And I'm sure Thunder would be glad to see you."

Thunder, a beautiful chestnut quarter horse, belonged to Ted Rogers, a stable boy at Carson Stable. Ted allowed Elizabeth to ride Thunder whenever she wanted to.

"I *do* miss him," Elizabeth said softly.

"Who?" Jessica asked with a sly smile. "Thunder, or Ted?"

"Thunder!" Elizabeth laughed. When the twins had first met Ted, who was a freshman at Sweet Valley High, Jessica had developed quite a crush on the shy, blue-eyed boy. Although he and Elizabeth were just friends, Jessica couldn't resist teasing her twin about him.

"Jessica! Look!" Elizabeth cried.

A magnificent black Arabian came trotting down the trail. His rider was a girl about the twins' age. She was wearing a black riding jacket, tan breeches, and a black velvet cap. As she passed the twins, she looked down and smiled.

"What beautiful conformation!" Elizabeth whispered as she watched the horse and rider disappear around a bend.

"Yeah, and that horse was pretty, too," Jessica agreed.

Elizabeth giggled. "That's what I *meant*, Jess."

"Oh." Jessica shrugged. "I thought you were talking about her outfit." She stood up and brushed off her shorts. "I never *did* understand all that horse talk. Conformation, hairycombs—"

"*Curry*combs," Elizabeth corrected.

"Whatever." Jessica waved her hand. "Are

you ready to go back? I'm in the mood for another piece of chocolate cake."

"More cake! I thought you were so full you couldn't move!"

"Full of hot dogs," Jessica explained. "I'm never too full for cake!"

As the girls headed back, Elizabeth couldn't take her mind off the beautiful Arabian horse they'd just seen. "Tomorrow, I'm going to visit Thunder," she said. "I've really missed him."

"You make it sound as if he's a *person*, Elizabeth."

"In a way, he is. To me, anyway," Elizabeth replied.

When they neared the picnic area, the twins caught sight of Mr. and Mrs. Wakefield and Steven, the twins' fourteen-year-old brother, playing Frisbee.

"Let's go play," Elizabeth suggested.

"I'll be right there, after I find the cake."

"Save me a piece!" Elizabeth called as she ran toward the shore.

As Jessica approached the Wakefields' picnic blanket, she was surprised to see the lid of their cooler slightly ajar.

"I could have sworn Mom closed that," she muttered as she pulled back the lid.

Jessica reached inside for the chocolate cake. Suddenly, she gasped in horror.

"A *skunk*!" she screamed at the top of her lungs. "Help, somebody!"

A baby skunk sat in the bottom of the cooler.

He looked up at Jessica, blinked his little black eyes, and returned to his chocolate cake.

"Jessica!" Mr. Wakefield called as he dashed toward her. "Honey, are you OK?"

"There's a skunk eating my chocolate cake!" Jessica cried, pointing toward the picnic blanket.

"A skunk?" Steven repeated as he raced up, followed by Mrs. Wakefield and Elizabeth. "Let's see!"

"Careful, Steven," Mr. Wakefield warned. "Wild animals can be dangerous. And we don't want to scare him." Cautiously Mr. Wakefield approached the cooler as the rest of the family gathered around.

The little skunk peered up at the Wakefields curiously. He took one last bite of cake, jumped out, and scampered toward the woods.

"There goes your cake thief, Jessica." Mr. Wakefield grinned.

"Wasn't he adorable!" Elizabeth exclaimed.

"Oh, *please*, Elizabeth," Jessica said in a disgusted voice. "I've had about enough of Mother Nature for one day."

Early the next afternoon, Elizabeth walked to Carson Stable. Her steps quickened when the huge redwood buildings, surrounded by lush, green pastures, came into view. Elizabeth took a deep breath of the sweet, familiar scent of horses and hay. She'd almost forgotten how much she loved those wonderful smells.

Elizabeth spotted Ted folding a saddle blanket

in the tack room, a wooden shed filled with everything from bridles and saddles to hoof picks and brushes. "Need a hand?" Elizabeth asked as she stepped inside.

"Elizabeth," Ted exclaimed. "Boy, it's good to see you." He smiled broadly. "It's been a long time! Thunder's really missed you and so have I," Ted added shyly.

"I'm going to say hello to him. Want to come along?"

"Sure," Ted replied. "I'm about finished in here, anyway."

When they reached the stable, Elizabeth moved down the long line of stalls, saying hello to all her old friends until she finally came to Thunder's stall.

"It's me, Thunder," Elizabeth cooed.

Thunder pricked up his ears at the sound of Elizabeth's voice. He stepped over to the stable door and rubbed his velvety-soft muzzle against Elizabeth's cheek.

"Look what I brought you, boy." Elizabeth reached into her jacket pocket and pulled out a piece of carrot. Thunder took it gently in his big teeth and munched away happily.

Elizabeth ran her hand along Thunder's strong, glistening neck. "Looks like Ted's been taking good care of you." Elizabeth turned to Ted. "I'm so glad you bought Thunder from Lila, Ted. You and he were meant to be together."

Lila Fowler was Jessica's closest friend and a member of the Unicorns. She was incredibly spoiled by her wealthy father. To make up for all the time Mr. Fowler spent traveling, he bought Lila anything she wanted. And for a time, Lila had wanted a horse. But as with most of her other possessions, almost as soon as she had Thunder, she grew bored with him. Fortunately, Ted had convinced Lila to sell him.

"I'm glad I bought Thunder, too." Suddenly, Ted frowned. "Of course, if I don't come up with some money very soon, I may not be able to keep him much longer."

"Ted, what do you mean?" Elizabeth asked anxiously.

Ted looked down at the floor. "It's the monthly payments to the stable for boarding Thunder. Even with my part-time job here, I haven't been able to keep up with the bills. Right now, I'm three months behind, and if I don't come up with the money soon, I'm going to have to sell Thunder."

"Ted! That would be *awful*!" Elizabeth cried.

Ted nodded grimly. "My dad's helped out as much as he can, but he doesn't earn much money. And it's *my* responsibility to take care of Thunder." He reached up and ran his fingers through Thunder's thick mane. "If I ever lost this guy, I don't know what I'd do," he whispered.

Elizabeth nodded sympathetically. She knew that Ted had already suffered enough painful loss. Two years before, Ted and his parents had been driving on the freeway when their car had been hit by a drunk driver. Ted's mother, an expert horsewoman, had been killed. Ted's leg had been badly hurt, and he still walked with a slight limp.

"We can't let you lose Thunder," Elizabeth said forcefully. "There has *got* to be a way to come up with the money."

"Actually, there is," Ted said, a smile returning to his face. "The regional junior jumping championship is in two weeks. If I win, I could use the prize money to pay for Thunder's boarding fees."

"That's right. Ellen Riteman told Jessica about the competition. And what do you mean, *'If'*?" Elizabeth exclaimed. "Of course you'll win!" Ted was the finest horseman she'd ever met.

Ted smiled self-consciously. "Well, I think I have a shot at it. But there are going to be some great riders competing and it's hard to get in as much practice as I'd like."

"I'll help you train, Ted," Elizabeth volunteered eagerly. "And I could help you with some of your work here at the stable, so you can have extra time to practice with Thunder."

"That would be great, Elizabeth," Ted said gratefully. Suddenly, his expression grew serious and he nodded toward the entrance. "Here comes Mr. Carson."

The gray-haired owner of the stable strode toward them and shook Ted's hand. "How's it going, Ted?"

"Hi, Mr. Carson. This is Elizabeth Wakefield."

Mr. Carson nodded at Elizabeth. "Haven't I seen you around here riding our friend Thunder?"

"Whenever I get the chance," Elizabeth replied.

Mr. Carson scratched Thunder's muzzle. "A fine horse, this one," he said. "I'd hate to see you lose him, Ted, but I'm afraid I've given you about all the time I can on the overdue payments."

Ted cleared his throat nervously. "I was hoping you could give me until the regional championships at the end of the month, Mr. Carson."

"The regionals, eh?" Mr. Carson rubbed his chin. "If anybody has a chance at winning, it's you and Thunder." Mr. Carson paused. "All right, Ted. I'll give you until the championship to come up with the back payments."

"Thanks, Mr. Carson," Ted said with a sigh of relief. "You won't be sorry."

"I hope not," Mr. Carson said kindly. "But that's all the time I can give you, understand?"

"Yes, sir."

"Practice hard, now. That's a tough competition," Mr. Carson warned. He gave Thunder one last pat and strode off.

"I've got to win, Elizabeth," Ted said with determination. "Everything depends on it."

Suddenly, a horse in one of the back stalls whinnied and shifted nervously. "Who was that?" Elizabeth asked.

"It sounded like Calypso," Ted replied. "He probably just wants to know if you have any more carrots."

"But I thought I heard a voice, too."

"As far as I know, Calypso hasn't learned to

speak yet," Ted said with a smile, "but let's go check it out."

Ted led Elizabeth to Calypso's stall. As they approached, the dappled gray pricked up his ears.

"He's got a piece of sugar in his mouth," Ted said in surprise. "You didn't give it to him, did you?"

Elizabeth shook her head.

"That's strange. I haven't seen anyone else around here." Ted pointed toward the door. "Let's check the riding ring."

But the ring was deserted. "Oh, well," Ted said with a shrug. "I've got enough on my mind right now without worrying about sugar cube fairies."

They returned to Thunder's stall and Elizabeth began to stroke the big horse's ears. "Don't worry, boy," she said. "You and Ted are going to win that competition! I know you will!"

Thunder dipped his head in a graceful nod as if to say, "Of course we will."

But when Elizabeth looked over at Ted, she could tell he wasn't quite so sure.

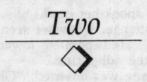

Two

"Look," Jessica exclaimed. "The whole beach seems deserted!"

When Elizabeth had left for the stable, Jessica had called Lila Fowler to see if she wanted to spend the day at the beach, and Lila had immediately agreed.

Jessica and Lila turned their bikes into the almost empty parking lot alongside the beach. "I was sure the beach would be jammed with people on a beautiful Sunday like this," Jessica said.

"Better for us," Lila said, tossing her head. "I hate it when the beach is crowded with little kids playing and kicking sand around. It's *so* hard to concentrate on relaxing."

"Maybe you should just ask your father to buy you your own private beach," Jessica joked.

Lila seemed to seriously consider the idea.

"Hmm, maybe you're right. When I get home, I'll ask—"

"Come on, Lila," Jessica interrupted. "It looks like we'll have plenty of privacy today—even for you."

The two girls unpacked their towels and a portable radio from their bike baskets. They took off their shoes and headed along the path that led from the parking lot to the beach.

"This is really weird," Jessica said as they made their way across the warm, white sand. "This place should be packed. Instead, it's like a ghost town."

"Maybe there was a shark and it scared everyone away!" Lila said excitedly. "We'd better not go into the water until we find out if it's safe."

"I don't know if it's a shark," Jessica said, crinkling her nose, "but something sure smells bad."

As they came closer to the water's edge, the smell grew even stronger. Then Jessica stared in disbelief. "Am I crazy, Lila," she murmured, squinting her eyes, "or is that wave the wrong color?"

Lila shaded her eyes with her hand and looked out over the water. "If you're crazy, I must be, too, Jessica. That wave is *definitely* black!"

The wave rolled in and crashed on the sand. As the water slipped back out to sea, it left behind a gooey, black layer of slime.

"Gross!" Lila screamed. "What is it?"

Jessica knelt down to examine the slimy substance. "I don't know. It smells a little like our garage." Gingerly, she stuck a finger in the slime. "It feels like tar."

"Well, how can we go swimming in this mess?" Lila demanded.

Jessica shrugged. "Maybe it's OK further down the beach. Let's head toward those people on the rocks ahead. Maybe they know what's going on."

As they trudged along the shore, the sticky black substance seemed to follow them. In some places the sand had been turned completely black. "It looks like someone came along and painted the whole beach," Jessica remarked angrily. "What a disgusting mess."

"See? This is why I need my own private beach," Lila complained. "Then no one could ruin my whole day like this."

The girls came to a jumble of large rocks that had been piled by the sea into a high barrier. Jessica had explored the rocks in calm weather. But at high tide, or when the ocean was stormy, they could be dangerous. "Even the rocks have goo all over them!" she cried.

A group of six people, most of them wearing T-shirts and shorts with heavy boots, was scattered across the rocks. They looked as if they were high school or college age, except for one boy who appeared to be only a year or two older than Jessica and Lila. He was wearing black and turquoise swim trunks and a white tank top. His hair was long and just a bit darker than Jessica's.

"I think we should try and find out what's going on," Jessica said.

"And I'll bet I can guess who you want to ask," Lila replied with a smile. "But I'm not about to climb up on those filthy rocks. I'll ruin my shorts and get my legs all dirty, too."

"Don't you want to know what happened to the beach?" Jessica asked.

"I don't *care* what happened to the beach," Lila pouted. "All I know is my day is ruined and now you want me to go climbing around and get dirty and probably skin my knees."

"Well, I'm going to try and catch up with those people. Are you coming or not?"

"Oh, all right," Lila said grumpily. "I don't want to be stranded here all by myself!"

"Good. I'll climb up first, then I'll pull you up after me."

But climbing wasn't as easy as Jessica had thought. Her feet kept slipping on the slimy surface of the rocks, and by the time she'd managed to get to the top of the first rock, her bare legs were streaked with black slime. "See?" she called to Lila, trying to sound confident. "That was easy!"

"If I ruin my shorts just so you can talk to some boy," Lila warned, "I'll never forgive you!" She reached up and took Jessica's hand. Jessica pulled hard and Lila scampered up beside her.

Just then the girls heard a strange noise, like the barking of a puppy. Jessica jumped in surprise, slipped, and fell into a pool of black muck.

"Ow!" Jessica cried. "Why did you make that noise, Lila? Look what you made me do!"

"*I* didn't make any noise," Lila protested. "I thought it was you!"

The barking noise came again, louder this time. Jessica looked over toward the group of people, but they were too far away either to have made the sound or to have heard it.

"I think it came from that direction," Lila said, indicating the point at which the rocks met the water. "It sounds like some kind of animal noise."

"I'm going to take a look."

"Don't go too near the water," Lila warned. "A wave could come along and sweep you away."

"I'll be careful," Jessica reassured her. She clambered over the slippery rocks, splashing through the little pools of blackened seawater that had collected in the hollows between boulders. The noise came again and Jessica realized it was coming from a crevice between two very large rocks.

Carefully, Jessica knelt down and peered into the dark space. Two big, black eyes stared back at her.

"Lila!" she called. "Come quick!"

"What is it?" Lila asked, as she stepped carefully across the rocks.

"I don't know. It's some kind of animal, and I think it's trapped in this hole."

"What *kind* of animal?" Lila asked suspiciously. "It's not a snake, is it?"

As Jessica looked down into its glistening dark eyes, the animal barked again. "I think it's a seal," she called out. "A baby seal."

"You shouldn't touch it." Lila knelt down beside Jessica and peered into the dark hole. "It could have rabies or something. What if it bites?"

"He looks pretty harmless to me," Jessica murmured.

"Well, you never can tell. You're better off just leaving it alone."

The seal barked again, but this time weakly.

"What if he's sick?" Jessica wondered. "What if I leave him here and he dies?"

"Wild animals know how to take care of themselves," Lila said. "Besides, since when did you become an animal lover?"

"I guess you're right," Jessica admitted, remembering her run-in with the baby skunk.

"Besides," Lila continued, "those people look like they're leaving, and I thought you wanted to ask them what happened to the beach."

Jessica stood up and sighed. She had only gone a few steps when the seal made a soft *krooh, krooh* sound, like the mooing of a hungry calf. The sound was so mournful that Jessica stopped in her tracks.

"Jessica!" Lila put her hands on her hips. "It's just a stupid seal!"

Jessica knew Lila was probably right. But then she thought of the huge, shining eyes that seemed to be asking for her help.

Suddenly she grabbed Lila by the arm. "I

have to save that seal! I can't just leave him there. You go ask those people what's going on. I'll catch up with you as soon as I pull him out of the hole and throw him back in the water."

"All right," Lila said with a sigh. "You play with your little animal friend, and *I'll* go talk with that guy in the white tank top. I thought he was cute, too."

As Lila carefully made her way across the rocks, Jessica returned to the seal. She got down on her knees and reached her hand into the hole. But the seal was farther down than he seemed, and Jessica was unable to reach him.

"Now, you'd better be *really* grateful! I'm going to have to totally destroy my outfit to save you!" Screwing up her face in disgust, Jessica lay flat on her stomach on the slimy, black rock and stretched her arm all the way down into the hole. At last she could feel the seal with her fingertips. His coat seemed to be covered with the same gooey substance that covered the rocks. The seal was small enough for her to get her hand around his back. Slowly, she began to pull him upward. Suddenly, the seal wiggled free.

"Talk about ungrateful!" Jessica muttered. She reached down again and grabbed hold of the seal, this time with both hands. "Now, I've got you," she said, as she carefully pulled the seal from the hole.

Jessica sat up and placed the seal pup in her lap. He was about as big as a house cat. His eyes were round and alert, and his whiskers were long and thick. He looked up at Jessica and whimpered sadly. "Don't be scared, little guy," Jessica murmured. "I'm not going to hurt you. I'm going to put you right back in the water so your mother can find you."

"I'm not so sure his mother will be able to find him."

Jessica turned and saw the boy she'd seen earlier. He had deep brown eyes that were a little like the seal's. Lila was standing behind him.

"Hi, my name's Adam," the boy said. "Adam Scott."

"I'm Jessica Wakefield." Jessica smiled. "I heard this little seal—"

"Actually," Lila said quickly, "*We* heard the seal, and *I* thought it would be nice if we could save it so—"

"So *I* laid down on this rock and got covered in this slime, or whatever it is," Jessica finished.

"It's oil," Adam said. "The stuff is all over these rocks and all over the beach. A tanker went aground last night and broke open. That must be how this little guy got separated from his mother. She probably lost him in the oil slick." Adam reached out and gently stroked the seal's head.

"Well, I'm certainly glad we were able to save it, Adam," Lila said.

Jessica rolled her eyes. "Yes, I'm glad that *I* saved Whiskers." She flashed a brilliant smile at Adam.

"Whiskers?" Lila echoed.

"That's his name," Jessica said. "While I was saving him, I decided to give him a name."

"Well, I don't know if Whiskers has really been saved yet or not," Adam said softly. "A wild animal this young may have a hard time surviving. I'll have to talk to Dr. Robinson and see what he thinks we should do."

"Dr. Robinson?" Jessica asked. "Who's he?"

"He's the head of our group. You see, we're all members of Ecology Now. That's an organization that works to protect the environment. We're going to be working here to try to clean up the oil," Adam explained. "Dr. Robinson is one of the marine biologists from the Sweet Valley Aquarium. He'll know what to do with Whiskers."

"How are you going to clean up all this mess?" Lila asked.

Adam grinned. "With an awful lot of hard, dirty work. I'll be coming here every day after school until we get it done. If either of you would like to help, we can always use volunteers."

"I'd *love* to, Adam," Lila said, "but I have such a busy social life . . . "

"I could help out," Jessica said quickly.

Lila looked at her as if she'd gone crazy, and Jessica wondered what she'd gotten herself into. The cleanup work would be messy and tiring, and she might even have to miss a Unicorn meeting—

"Great!" Adam smiled at Jessica, and all at once the idea of cleaning up oil sludge seemed more attractive.

"I can't wait to get started," Jessica said, returning Adam's smile.

Lila sighed loudly.

"Now let's take Whiskers over to see Dr. Robinson," Adam said. "I sure hope we can save this little guy."

Three

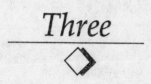

"Where is everybody?" Jessica shouted as she closed the front door behind her.

The Wakefields were gathered in front of the television in the den. "Jessica!" Elizabeth exclaimed. "You won't believe what happened today!"

"Oh, yes I will," Jessica said grimly. "I saw it myself."

Mr. Wakefield turned down the volume on the TV. "We were just watching a special report about the oil spill," he explained. "How bad did the beach look?"

"Horrible," Jessica reported. "There was black goop everywhere!"

"What did you do?" Steven asked, pointing to Jessica's dirty clothes. "Roll in it?"

"For your information, I saved a life," Jessica retorted.

"Honey, what happened?" Mrs. Wakefield cried. "Was someone drowning?"

"Well, not exactly *someone*. He's more like a *something*." Jessica paused dramatically. "He's a baby seal."

"Give me a break," Steven scoffed. "You don't even like dogs, and we're supposed to believe you saved a seal?"

"Well, he would have died, if I hadn't found him," Jessica said defensively. "At least, that's what Dr. Robinson said."

"Who's Dr. Robinson?" Mrs. Wakefield asked.

"He's from the Sweet Valley Aquarium. I guess he's sort of a vet. He was at the beach with some other people working on the cleanup. Dr. Robinson said Whiskers had so much oil on his coat that he wouldn't have lived long if I hadn't found him when I did."

"Whiskers?" Elizabeth repeated.

"That's what I named him," Jessica said. "Wait until you see him, Lizzie. He has the cutest little face, and big brown eyes."

"Is he going to be OK?" Elizabeth asked.

Jessica shook her head. "Nobody knows for sure. He was awfully weak. I'm going to go back to the beach tomorrow to help with the cleanup. Dr. Robinson may know more by then."

"Wait a minute." Steven narrowed his eyes. "*You're* going to help with the cleanup?"

"That's what I said, Steven," Jessica snapped. "Do you need a hearing aid or something?"

"What's the catch?" Steven pressed. "They're paying you, right?"

"Steven, I think it's wonderful that your sister's taking an interest in the environment," Mrs. Wakefield said.

"That's right, Steven," Mr. Wakefield said sternly. "You should be proud that Jessica's going to take part in the cleanup effort."

"But she won't even clean up her *room!*" Steven exclaimed.

"I wish I could help out," Elizabeth said earnestly. "But I promised Ted Rogers I'd help him train for the regional jumping championships every day after school."

"When are the championships?" Jessica asked.

"The end of the month."

"Well, from what I heard today, there will still be plenty of oil around then," Jessica said. "Adam said the cleanup could go on for weeks."

"Wait a minute." Steven grinned. "Who's Adam?"

"Just a boy," Jessica answered, studying a smudge of oil on her hand.

"I *knew* there was a catch," Steven said with a laugh.

On Monday, everyone at Sweet Valley Middle School was talking about the oil spill.

"You're not actually going to help with the cleanup this afternoon, are you?" Lila asked Jessica as they sat down at the Unicorner, the Unicorns' favorite table in the lunch room.

"Of course I am," Jessica replied. But the truth was, she wasn't feeling as enthusiastic about the cleanup effort today as she had yesterday afternoon. Adam was cute, but Jessica wasn't sure that he was reason enough for her to spend her free time ankle-deep in black sludge. Besides, Aaron Dallas, a boy she knew at Sweet Valley Middle School, was cuter.

"You haven't forgotten about the Boosters practice this afternoon, have you?" asked Ellen Riteman. The Boosters was a cheering and baton squad organized by the Unicorns.

It was the perfect excuse. She couldn't be in two places at the same time, could she?

"I forgot all about practice," Jessica said, shaking her head regretfully. "And I really wanted to go straight to the beach after school to help out."

"*Sure* you did," Lila said skeptically. "Well, maybe you'll see Whiskers at the aquarium when we go on the field trip Tuesday." Each class was going to visit the aquarium so that the students could learn what effects the oil spill had had on local marine life. "And you can always see Adam another day," Lila added.

"You're as bad as Steven!" Jessica exclaimed. "You think I'm only interested in Whiskers because of Adam!"

Lila pretended to be horrified. "*Me?* Where would I ever get an idea like that?"

"Who's Whiskers?" Ellen asked as she tore open a bag of potato chips.

"Jessica's pet seal," Lila answered.

"You have your own *seal*?" Ellen asked doubtfully. "Where do you keep him? In the pool?"

"No, Ellen, in the bathtub," Jessica said in an exasperated voice.

"Jess!" A voice called.

Jessica twisted around to see Elizabeth approaching. "Hi, Elizabeth," she said, grateful for the interruption. "What's up?"

"I just wanted to remind you that I'm going straight to the stable after school, so I won't be walking home with you," Elizabeth said.

"That's OK," Jessica replied. "I just remembered that I have a Boosters practice after school."

"What about the cleanup?"

Jessica frowned. It figured Elizabeth would make her feel guilty about breaking her promise. "I've got a brand-new baton routine to learn," Jessica explained quickly.

"You know, Jessica," Lila said with a smirk, "I could always teach you the routine later."

"Thanks anyway, Lila," Jessica snapped. "So when will you get home from the stable?" she asked Elizabeth, trying to change the subject.

"Probably pretty late," Elizabeth replied. "I want to help Ted as long as I can."

"Ted Rogers?" Ellen asked.

Elizabeth nodded. "I'm going to help out at the stable so Ted can have more time to practice for the regionals."

"He's been helping Snow White and me with our jumps," Ellen said. "I'm entering the championship in the junior hunters class. Ted says we have a good chance at a blue ribbon."

"It sounds as if the competition's going to be tough," Elizabeth said.

Ellen shrugged. "Nothing I can't handle."

"Have you been practicing a lot?" Elizabeth asked.

"Enough," Ellen answered confidently. "There's such a thing as *over*training, you know. I want to be fresh for the competition."

"Ted says he's been practicing with Thunder every spare minute he has," Elizabeth said.

"You'd better not get overconfident, Ellen," Lila warned. "Someone might just come along and surprise you."

"That'll be the day!" Ellen laughed but Jessica thought she looked just a little worried.

"Ellen Riteman seems pretty confident about winning in the junior hunters competition," Elizabeth told Ted that afternoon as she helped him sweep out the feed room.

"Ellen's not a bad rider," Ted said thoughtfully. "Not as good as *you*," he added with a wink. "But I think she has a good shot at winning if she practices hard. In fact, in a year or two, she might be ready to challenge me on the junior jumpers. Of course, then I won't want to help her practice."

"Speaking of practicing," Elizabeth said, "I'll take care of sweeping up the stable, if you want to go work out with Thunder."

Ted smiled gratefully. "You're something else, Elizabeth Wakefield. How am I ever going to repay you?"

"By winning that blue ribbon!" Elizabeth exclaimed. "Don't forget that I have my own reasons for helping you out, Ted. I love Thunder almost as much as you do! And I can't wait to ride him today after I finish with work."

Carrying her broom, Elizabeth followed Ted to the stable. When they got to Thunder's stall, they found him crunching loudly on a piece of carrot. "When did you sneak away to feed him?" Ted asked.

"I didn't." Elizabeth leaned her broom against the door of Thunder's stall and began to walk the length of the stable. "Hey, Ted, it looks like just about everybody's had a visit from the Carrot Fairy."

Ted put his hands on his hips. "This is really weird," he said. "Let's check outside and see if we can get to the bottom of this mystery."

But the area immediately outside the stable was deserted. Elizabeth and Ted headed toward the ring, where a class of beginning riders was circling at a walk.

"Nobody unusual here, either," Ted said. "Guess the identity of the Carrot Fairy will have to remain a mystery."

"Wait a minute. See that girl leaning against the fence on the far side of the ring?" Elizabeth pointed to a slender girl with curly black shoulder-length hair. "I think I've seen her at school. But I've never seen her here before. Have you?"

Ted shook his head. "And see the way she's watching us? She looks a little guilty, if you ask me. Let's go see what she's up to."

As Ted and Elizabeth approached the girl, her cheeks flushed bright pink.

"Hi," Ted said. "Are you waiting for a riding lesson?"

"Um, no," the girl mumbled. "I was just, uh, watching."

"My name's Ted Rogers, and this is Elizabeth Wakefield."

"I'm Lucy," the girl said shyly. "Lucy Benson."

Elizabeth caught Ted's eye and nodded toward the book bag on the ground by Lucy's feet. Poking out of the top were several carrots.

"I think we may have found our Carrot Fairy, Elizabeth," Ted said with a grin.

Lucy glanced down at her book bag and her face grew even redder. "I—I'm sorry," she stammered. "I just wanted to say hello to the horses."

"Do you ride?" Elizabeth asked.

Lucy nodded.

"Have you ridden long?" Elizabeth pressed.

"Since I was seven," Lucy answered softly. She nodded at the riders posting awkwardly at a slow trot around the ring. "I was younger than most of them when I started."

"You must be very good." Although Lucy seemed very shy, Elizabeth could see her brown eyes light up with enthusiasm as she watched the horses.

"I'm a good rider," Lucy said simply. But something in her voice sounded uncertain.

"Do you own a horse?" Ted asked.

Lucy shook her head slowly. "Not anymore. I had a beautiful bay thoroughbred."

"What was his name?" Ted wanted to know.

"Starfire. He had a perfect white star on his forehead."

"You're so lucky. I'd love to have my own horse." Elizabeth wanted to ask what had happened to Starfire, but the sad look in Lucy's eyes made her hesitate.

"Ted lets me ride his horse, Thunder, whenever I want," Elizabeth continued.

"Thunder's *yours*?" Lucy asked Ted excitedly. "He's incredible! He's so spirited and intelligent."

Ted smiled proudly. "It sounds as if you two have already gotten acquainted."

"Oh, I know all the horses here," Lucy told him. "I know that Calypso's a little skittish, but he'll do anything for a piece of sugar. Gypsy loves it when you scratch behind her right ear. And, let's see . . . Big Red's sweet as can be, but he's a bit of a hayburner."

"Hey, I've got an idea!" Elizabeth exclaimed. "I'm helping Ted with his work at the stable so he can have more time to train for the regional championships at the end of the month. Now I remember. I *have* seen you at school. Why don't we meet when classes are over? We can both come by and help Ted."

"That would be great!" Lucy said shyly.

"Just be sure you bring a big supply of carrots," Ted reminded her. "I'm sure the horses would be awfully disappointed if the Carrot Fairy didn't show up!"

"I promise," Lucy said.

"Why don't you take Thunder out for a quick ride?" Ted suggested.

"You mean . . . *now*?" Lucy's face grew pale.

"Sure," Ted replied. "I've got plenty of time to practice."

"You won't believe how responsive he is," Elizabeth urged. "When I ride Thunder, I feel as if I'm floating on air!"

Lucy glanced nervously at her watch. "I'd really love to," she said. "But I've got a ton of homework." She picked up her book bag and took a few steps backward. "Thanks for the offer, though, Ted. Maybe I can take you up on it some other time." Without another word, Lucy spun on her heel and ran off.

"Well, at least we solved the great carrot question," Ted said with a smile.

That's one question answered, anyway, Elizabeth thought to herself as she watched Lucy depart.

Four

◇

"I expect you all to be on your best behavior at the aquarium," warned Mr. Tilley, the head of the science department at Sweet Valley Middle School. He stood at the front of the crowded bus, trying to be heard over the static in his microphone. "That means quiet with a capital 'Q.' And there's to be absolutely *no* touching or feeding the animals."

Seated next to Jessica, Lila didn't seem very interested in anything Mr. Tilley had to say. "Oh, Jessica, I almost forget to tell you about my dad's surprise!"

"Let me guess—he bought you a Mercedes," Jessica said sarcastically.

"No."

"He wants you to get a job at Burger Town so you can start paying for your own clothes?"

"Oh, Jessica, *please*." Lila rolled her eyes.

"He's got a big surprise for me, and the only clue he'll give me is that everybody is going to be incredibly jealous when they find out what it is. I'll bet even Brooke Dennis will be impressed, even though her father *did* throw that fabulous party."

Now it was Jessica's turn to roll her eyes. Sometimes Lila was just too much.

Jessica turned to Elizabeth, who was sitting across the aisle with Amy Sutton. "I wonder if I'll see Whiskers?"

But before Elizabeth could respond, the bus jerked to a stop and everyone ran for the exit.

As Elizabeth left the bus she noticed Lucy Benson in a crowd of students already at the entrance to the aquarium. "Wait for me, will you?" she asked Amy. "I'm going to say hi to someone."

When Lucy caught sight of Elizabeth approaching, her expression darkened. She said something to the two girls she was with and ran to meet Elizabeth.

"Hi, Lucy," Elizabeth said. "Looks like practically the whole school's here today, huh?"

Lucy nodded. "It's funny. We hardly ever see each other at school but we meet at the aquarium." She smiled nervously.

"Actually, I just wanted to see if you were planning on going back to the stable this afternoon."

Lucy glanced around anxiously.

"Is something wrong?" Elizabeth asked.

"What? Oh, no," Lucy answered quickly.

"So will you be there?"

Lucy nodded. "I'll see you this afternoon, Elizabeth." And without another word, she dashed off.

Elizabeth rejoined her classmates who were already gathered in the lobby of the aquarium.

"I'm your guide, and I'd like to welcome you all to the Sweet Valley Aquarium," said a young woman. She was wearing jeans and her long hair was braided down her back.

"Here at the aquarium we're caring for many birds and sea mammals who were caught in the devastating oil spill this past weekend. As you know, over a mile of shoreline was affected by the oil, and the cleanup efforts may take months."

She led the group into a large fenced-in outdoor area in the rear of the aquarium.

Small wire cages were stacked up in rows. Many contained birds who rested on perches or pecked at bowls of bird seed. Some were clean, but others were still coated with oil. Two men and a woman were cleaning the birds one by one in a big, steel tub filled with water.

"All of these birds were covered with oil from the spill," the guide said. "We clean some of them right at the beach, but others must be brought here. If the birds aren't cleaned quickly, the oil will affect their ability to resist cold water, and they may get too cold and die."

The guide led them toward a second cleaning tank. "Over here we have an otter we've named

Joey. Joey was also covered in oil, and oil has the same effect on otters that it does on birds. In fact, we were unable to save one of Joey's brothers, who died here just this morning."

The news made Jessica very anxious. She had assumed that once Whiskers made it safely to the aquarium, he would be all right.

The class moved on to a shallow cement tank that looked like a wading pool. Standing nearby was Dr. Robinson. In the pool, Jessica could see the tiny, spotted figure of Whiskers.

"Dr. Robinson will tell you about one of our youngest favorites here at the aquarium," said the guide with a smile.

"This little guy is named Whiskers," Dr. Robinson began. "He is a young harbor seal who was found by—as a matter of fact," he said, peering at the class, "I believe the girl who saved Whiskers is here today. At least, *one* of you is the girl. I'm sorry, but I can't tell you apart."

"It was me." Jessica held up her hand and beamed.

"Well, you're all here just in time to see Whiskers get his fish milk shake." Dr. Robinson signaled to the guide, who bent down and picked Whiskers up from the pool. Then she picked up a baby bottle that stood on a nearby table.

"We feed the baby seal on a formula similar to its mother's milk. It's made of ground-up herring and whipped cream," Dr. Robinson explained.

While the guide held Whiskers, Dr. Robinson

poked the bottle into the seal's mouth. Whiskers sniffed at the bottle, but he took only a small sip.

Dr. Robinson sighed. "We would like to get Whiskers to eat more. He's still very weak from his ordeal. Maybe after he gets used to us, he'll develop more of an appetite. We're worried that he may have gotten some of the oil into his system. Oil contains toxic substances—poisons—that may still make him sick."

"But he'll be all right, won't he?" Jessica asked anxiously.

"I'm afraid we just don't know," Dr. Robinson said gravely. "We won't be sure for a couple of weeks. But we'll certainly do our best." He smiled at Jessica. "Would you like to try to feed him?"

Jessica stepped forward, aware that all of her classmates were watching her. She took the bottle from Dr. Robinson's hand and put it to Whisker's mouth. The seal looked up at her with its big, sad eyes and began sucking the fish milkshake happily.

Dr. Robinson laughed. "Well, maybe he just doesn't like *me* to feed him!"

Later, after the students had completed their tour of the aquarium and they were heading back to their busses, Jessica found that she couldn't get Whiskers' sad little face out of her mind. "He looked so helpless," she murmured to Elizabeth.

"I'm sure he'll be OK," Elizabeth said, but Jessica could see the doubt in her eyes.

Just as Jessica began climbing into the bus, she heard someone call her name.

"Hey, Jessica Wakefield! Over here!"

Jessica scanned the aquarium parking lot. "It's Adam!" she cried. "Don't let the bus driver go without me, Elizabeth."

Jessica dashed over to the bike rack where Adam was locking his bike. "Adam!" she said breathlessly. "What are you doing here?"

"We got out of school a little early today for teachers' conferences. I told Dr. Robinson I'd stop by to see if he could use any help. Why are you here?"

"We were touring the aquarium," Jessica explained. "And I saw Whiskers, Adam! He looks horrible!"

"I know." Adam nodded grimly. "It doesn't look good for the poor little guy."

"I feel so *awful* for him."

"All we can do is keep our fingers crossed," Adam told her in a comforting voice. "Say, where were you yesterday? I was hoping I'd see you down at the beach."

"Oh. I had a, uh—an emergency," Jessica said quickly. *A baton emergency*, she added to herself. Somehow she couldn't quite bring herself to tell Adam that she thought Boosters practice was more important than saving the environment.

"Well, maybe you can stop by this afternoon," Adam suggested. "We can use all the help we can get."

"Will you be there?" Jessica asked with a smile.

"After I get done here."

"I'll see you in a little while, then." *It's a dirty job, but someone's got to do it!* Jessica thought to herself. *And as long as Adam's there, it might as well be me!*

By the time Elizabeth got to the stable later that afternoon, Lucy was already hard at work in the tack room.

"I see Ted put you right to work!" Elizabeth exclaimed as she entered the tack room.

"Oh, I *asked* if I could clean the saddles," Lucy said with a self-conscious smile. "I know it sounds crazy, but I love this kind of work."

"I guess that means we're both crazy." Elizabeth laughed and set down her book bag. "I love it too."

"Lucky for me." came Ted's voice from the doorway. "Wow! You're almost done with that saddle."

"Do you have another one I could do?" Lucy asked eagerly.

Ted shook his head in amazement. "With you two helping me out like this, I won't have any excuse not to win the regionals."

"You'll win, all right," Lucy said confidently. Seeing Ted's surprised look, she added, "I've watched you ride. You and Thunder make a great team."

"Have you ever won a competition, Lucy?" Elizabeth asked.

Lucy looked down at the saddle she was cleaning and shrugged. "I've won a few," she mumbled. "But that was a long time ago."

"Ted? Are you ready to help me with my jumps?" Ellen Riteman had appeared in the doorway. She was wearing beige riding breeches, a beige turtleneck sweater, and shiny black boots that looked brand-new. Her short brown hair was pulled into a small ponytail.

"This is Lucy Benson," Ted said. "Lucy, meet Ellen Riteman, Snow White's owner."

"Hi," Lucy said shyly. "Snow White's a beautiful horse."

"I know," Ellen responded. "What grade are you in, anyway? I've never seen you around."

"Seventh. My family just moved to Sweet Valley a couple of months ago. I lived in Grove Hills before that. It's about fifty miles north of here."

"That's nice," Ellen said in a disinterested voice. She turned her full attention back to Ted and batted her blue eyes flirtatiously. "So are you coming, Ted, or do I have to drag you out of this tack room?"

"I promised Ellen I'd give her some pointers," Ted said to Lucy and Elizabeth. "Want to come along?"

"I'm not quite done here," Lucy said.

"The saddle can wait," Ted assured her.

"Come and watch," Ellen urged. "I'll show you how a pro rides."

The group headed to where Ellen had tied her horse. Ellen mounted Snow White and walked her to the center ring, while Ted, Lucy, and Elizabeth climbed onto the fence to watch.

"Blue ribbon, here I come!" Ellen called as she trotted Snow White around the ring. Snow White held her regal head high in the air, and Ellen smiled confidently as she passed her three spectators.

"She does fine with the lower post-and-rails," Ted whispered, pointing toward the smallest jumps in the ring. "But the others have been giving her trouble lately. Ellen's going to be in the junior hunters category, which is just below my event— junior jumper."

Ellen signaled Snow White, and they cleared the first three jumps effortlessly. But as she approached the next jump, Snow White suddenly veered to one side and trotted right past it.

"She just won't *obey* me!" Ellen cried in frustration as she yanked on the reins and brought the horse to a sudden halt.

"Just relax, Ellen," Ted advised. "And be sure to hold her in tight till you hit your spot."

Ellen rolled her eyes. "Come on, Snow," she grumbled. "And you had better get it right this time, or I'll trade you in for a new model."

Again Snow White took the first three jumps successfully, floating gracefully through the air. And again she refused the next jump.

"That does it!" Ellen shouted as she slowed Snow White to a walk.

"Ellen, it takes practice," Ted reminded her gently. "Snow's got to feel comfortable in the ring with you, or she's going to keep refusing jumps."

"It's not *my* fault she's stubborn!" Ellen cried. She gave Snow White a sharp kick and they cantered out of the ring.

Ted shook his head. "Ellen's not exactly the most patient rider I've ever met," he said.

"Poor Snow," Elizabeth said. "It's really not her fault. She's just not very comfortable jumping with Ellen yet."

"You know, I had the same problem with Starfire when I first started jumping," Lucy remarked. "It turned out to be more my fault than his."

"What do you mean?" Elizabeth asked.

"Well, it seems I was seated too far back in the saddle. Once I adjusted my posture, he had no problem."

"Maybe you should tell Ellen," Elizabeth suggested. "It might help her with Snow White."

The group headed to the stable where they found Ellen muttering under her breath as she unbridled Snow White.

"Hey, Ellen," Ted said. "We were just talking to Lucy, and she said she used to have the same problem you've been having."

"*I* don't have a problem," Ellen snapped. "My *horse* does."

"Starfire used to refuse, too, when I first

started jumping," Lucy said. "But then I realized—"

"What makes *you* such an expert, anyway?" Ellen interrupted.

"Lucy's won ribbons in competition, Ellen," Elizabeth said, coming to the defense of her new friend.

"*Sure* she has." Ellen crossed her arms over her chest and glared at Lucy. "If you're such a hotshot rider, why don't you just prove it to us? *You* take Snow in the ring and show us your blue ribbon form!"

Lucy's cheeks flamed. She stared at Snow White and her lower lip began to tremble slightly. "I would . . ." she began, letting her voice trail off.

"But what?" Ellen prodded. "But you've never been on a horse in your life?"

"No!" Lucy answered forcefully. "I *love* to ride." She looked at Elizabeth helplessly. "And I'm a good rider, really I am."

"I'm sure you are, Lucy," Elizabeth said kindly.

Lucy stepped over to Snow White and stroked the horse's soft muzzle. "Would you like to go for a ride, girl?" she whispered.

"Well?" Ellen said. "Are you going to ride or not?"

Lucy stared at Ellen and shook her head, almost as if she were trying to clear her mind of a troubling thought. "I'd like to, Ellen," she said at last. "But it's getting late and I have to finish cleaning that saddle. Maybe some other time."

"That's what I thought," Ellen said in a superior tone, as Lucy walked out of the stable.

"If I were you, I'd listen when people try to offer you advice, Ellen," Ted warned.

"When I need help, I'll ask for it," Ellen snapped.

Elizabeth ran to catch up with Lucy. She found Lucy in the tack room, rubbing the saddle she'd cleaned to a soft shine.

"Don't let Ellen bother you, Lucy," Elizabeth advised. "She's always that way."

"I guess I looked kind of stupid, didn't I?" Lucy's brown eyes were misty with tears.

"Not at all," Elizabeth reassured her. "If you don't want to ride, that's your business."

"It's not that I don't *want* to ride."

"What is it, then?" Elizabeth didn't want to pry, but she had the feeling Lucy needed to talk to someone.

Lucy opened her mouth to speak, but suddenly seemed to change her mind. "What do you think?" she asked, holding up the saddle for Elizabeth's inspection.

"It looks great." *If anything's bothering Lucy, she definitely doesn't want to talk about it,* Elizabeth thought to herself.

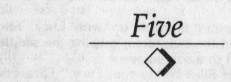

Five

◇

"There they go after another one!" Adam said excitedly, pointing out toward the water.

Jessica looked up and saw two of the older cleanup volunteers jump off the rocks into the black, oily water. Slowly they waded out to the spot where a seagull sat stranded. The bird tried to flap its wings, but they were so coated in the black, sticky substance that he could hardly move.

"That happens all the time," Adam explained. "The birds can't tell that the water's polluted. When they land on its surface, the oil coats their feathers so they can't fly away again. Then they freeze to death, because the oil destroys their natural insulation."

"At the aquarium today, the guide told us they had already saved hundreds of birds and animals," Jessica said.

"But there are plenty the volunteers can't reach in time," Adam said sadly.

"Then let's get going!" Jessica cried. "What should I do? I can work for at least an hour."

Adam laughed. "You'll need to work for weeks. And *this* is really a pretty small oil spill."

Weeks of hard work in slimy black goop wasn't exactly Jessica's idea of a good time. But if she could do something to help save other animals like Whiskers, it would be worth the trouble. Besides, Adam was pretty cute. And maybe she wouldn't actually have to touch any of the goop.

"What exactly do I have to do?" she asked Adam.

"Well, we're supposed to scrape some of the thicker oil off the rocks. Then later on, some experts with expertise will come in and steam clean them." Adam cocked his head and gave Jessica a doubtful look. "I don't know about your outfit, Jessica."

"Don't you like it?" Jessica asked innocently.

"Oh, yes," Adam answered quickly. "You look great. It's just that you're going to get all dirty. You'd be better off wearing a crummy pair of jeans and an old shirt."

"That's OK. I'll be fine," Jessica said, flipping her hair back over her shoulder.

Twenty minutes later, Jessica had to admit that Adam was right. She should have worn old clothes. Her legs were smeared with oil, and her shorts and shirt were ruined.

Both Adam and Jessica had a pile of rags and a scraper which they used to collect the oil off the rocks. Then they deposited the oil into cans. The cans would be emptied into barrels by other volunteers. When they were full, the barrels would be hauled away in trucks.

"This stuff reminds me of chewing gum," Jessica remarked, staring into Adam's collection can. "You know—when it sticks to the bottom of your shoe on a hot day?"

"Only this is a lot more dangerous," Adam said.

"I'd like to get my hands on whoever is responsible for this!" Jessica fumed. "I'm a total mess!"

"You look good to me," Adam said shyly. "Besides, it's easy to clean up a person. Cleaning up 10,000 barrels of oil off this beach—now *that's* a lot harder to do!"

Jessica was so pleased with Adam's compliment that it took a minute for the rest of what he'd said to register. "Wait a minute," she said, frowning. "Did you say 10,000? *Ten thousand barrels of oil?*" She gazed around her hopelessly. "But we haven't even filled half of *one* barrel yet!"

Adam wiped the perspiration from his forehead. "Yeah, it's a lot of work, all right." He smiled at Jessica. "I guess we'll be seeing a lot of each other here."

Jessica picked up an oily rag and sighed. Adam had a wonderful smile. And he *was* an eighth-grader. But Aaron's smile was even nicer. And 10,000 barrels was a lot to clean up.

For a minute she wondered whether anybody—even Adam and Whiskers—was worth that much work!

"Don't you *dare* throw that can in the trash, Steven Wakefield!" Jessica said loudly.

Steven paused, holding an empty soda can over the kitchen trash. "Why not?" he demanded.

"Because it's made out of aluminum and you can recycle it, that's why."

Steven looked at Jessica suspiciously. "Is this some kind of a joke?"

"I'll have you know that saving our environment is not a joke!" Jessica said hotly.

"I thought you were going to help me set the table, Jessica." Elizabeth said as she came into the kitchen.

"She's too busy bugging me," Steven said in an exasperated voice. He tossed the soda can to Jessica. "Here. It's all yours."

"Have you seen the paper napkins?" Elizabeth asked.

"Paper napkins? Elizabeth, how could you?" Jessica cried. "Don't you know that millions of trees get cut down every year to make paper? I think we should use cloth napkins. And—"

"Does this mean you're not going to help me set the table?" Elizabeth interrupted with a grin.

"Elizabeth! I thought that I could at least count on *you* to be interested in saving the world."

"Who's saving the world?" Mrs. Wakefield asked, joining them in the kitchen. She bent down and opened the oven door.

"Jessica is suddenly an ecology nut," Steven said. "Which means she's a boy nut!"

"I'm just trying to protect our environment," Jessica said defensively. "Adam says—"

"See?" Steven interrupted. "What did I tell you?"

Mrs. Wakefield lifted a roast from the oven and set it on the counter. "What did you want to do, Jessica?"

"Recycle our garbage, for one thing," Jessica explained. "We just have to buy separate holders for things like aluminum cans, newspapers, and glass bottles. Then we could take them to the recycling center."

Mrs. Wakefield nodded. "Well, it sounds like a good idea to me."

"I think it's a great idea, too, Jess," Elizabeth said enthusiastically.

"But, Mom," Steven protested, "Jessica's just doing this to impress her new boyfriend."

"He is *not* my boyfriend," Jessica insisted.

"Steven, it doesn't matter where the idea came from. The fact is, it's a good one. Recycling is a great way to do our part to help the environment." Mrs. Wakefield smiled at Jessica. "And I know just where we can start collecting aluminum cans!"

"Where?" Jessica asked eagerly.

"Under your bed!" Mrs. Wakefield said with a laugh.

On Wednesday, Elizabeth went straight to Carson Stable after school. She arrived to find Ted practicing his jumps in the ring. Ellen was standing by the fence with some of the stable workers watching Ted, but Lucy was nowhere in sight.

Ellen probably scared her off, Elizabeth thought in annoyance.

Reluctantly, Elizabeth joined Ellen. "He looks great, doesn't he?" Elizabeth said. "I just know Ted and Thunder are going to win!"

Ellen nodded. "I wish Snow White could do that." Her voice sounded almost wistful, and for a moment Elizabeth forgot her anger over the way Ellen had treated Lucy.

"With a little practice, you'll be great," Elizabeth said.

Ellen made a face. "Practicing gets so *boring*, though. If you've done one jump, you've done them all."

"I never get tired of riding Thunder," Elizabeth said, watching the great horse sail effortlessly over a tall post-and-rail.

"That's because he's not really yours," Ellen pointed out. "I *have* to ride Snow, or my parents will decide she was a waste of money and sell her." Suddenly she gestured toward the path leading to the stable. "Isn't that your friend, the riding expert?"

Elizabeth waved Lucy over. "She was only trying to help, Ellen," Elizabeth said sharply.

"Hi, you guys," Lucy said softly as she approached the fence. She smiled at Elizabeth but avoided Ellen's gaze.

"Look at Ted and Thunder," Elizabeth said. "They make it look so easy!"

"I just wish Ted would finish up so he could help me," Ellen complained. "He's been in the ring forever."

"Ellen, it's very important for Ted to win this competition," Elizabeth reminded her.

"Oh, I know all about it." Ellen waved her hand in the air. "He's behind on his rent payments to the stable and he might have to sell Thunder. Personally, I don't see why he just doesn't ask his father for the money."

Elizabeth groaned. "Maybe he can't afford to help Ted, Ellen. Did you ever think of that?"

"Do you think Ted might really have to sell Thunder?" Lucy asked anxiously.

Elizabeth nodded grimly. "He only has until the competition to come up with the money."

"How awful!" Lucy cried. She looked as though she might cry.

"Why are you getting so upset?" Ellen asked casually. "It's not *your* horse."

"It's just that I know . . . I can imagine what it would be like to have to sell an animal you love," Lucy explained. "Poor Ted!"

The girls watched Ted and Thunder trot around the ring. On their final jump, Thunder's rear hooves knocked a post just hard enough to send it toppling to the ground.

Elizabeth and Lucy ducked through the openings in the fence and ran into the ring to set up the post. "Try again, Ted!" Elizabeth called when they'd rejoined Ellen.

But when they circled around the ring a second time, Thunder's rear hooves grazed the post and again it fell to the ground.

"I don't know why we're having trouble with that jump," Ted said as he slowed Thunder to a walk and headed over to the girls. "We didn't have any problem with it yesterday."

"Maybe Thunder's getting tired," Elizabeth suggested. She reached over the fence to give the horse an affectionate pat.

Ted shook his head. "We're just getting warmed up."

"Just to be on the safe side, maybe you should let Thunder take a break. You could help me for a while," Ellen said sweetly.

"Maybe you're right, Ellen," Ted agreed.

"It was cloudy yesterday, wasn't it?" Lucy asked suddenly.

"It was overcast most of the day," Ted answered. "Why?"

"Well, it's probably a dumb theory—" Lucy began.

"Probably," Ellen interrupted.

"Go ahead, Lucy," Elizabeth urged.

Lucy took a breath. "It's just that I've noticed that on a sunny day like today, the sun can cast shadows across the approach to a jump. Sometimes the shadows will spook a horse, or he'll see a false ground line. If he can't judge the line at the base of the fence accurately, he'll jump too close. You have to guide him properly."

Ted turned around and gazed at the troublesome jump. Sure enough, there was a long shadow cast by the bright afternoon sun. "Lucy, you're a genius!" he cried. "I'll bet that's exactly what's happening!" He stroked Thunder's neck. "Come on, boy. Let's give that fence another shot!"

"What about me?" Ellen cried. "I thought you were going to take a break!"

"Later, Ellen," Ted said. "Right now I want to test Lucy's theory."

Ellen sighed dramatically. A moment later, Ted and Thunder flew over the post with inches to spare.

"Lucy, you're wonderful!" Ted called as Thunder trotted proudly around the ring.

Lucy flushed at his compliment.

"That was great, Lucy," Elizabeth said with admiration.

Only Ellen seemed unimpressed. "I still say you're all talk. I've seen everyone else around here ride except you."

"Ellen, it's obvious that Lucy knows a lot about horses," Elizabeth pointed out.

"That doesn't mean she knows how to *ride* one. Maybe she just likes to read horse books," Ellen argued.

"I do *so* know how to ride!" Lucy said hotly. "I'm a better rider than you'll *ever* be, Ellen!"

"OK. Prove it," Ellen challenged.

Lucy set her mouth in a grim line. She looked from Ellen to Elizabeth and then to Thunder. "Ted," she called, her voice quivering with anger, "may I borrow Thunder for a few minutes?"

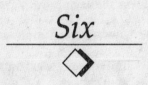

Six

Ted trotted Thunder over to the fence. "Sure," he said. "But why?"

Lucy slipped back through the fence. "I've got something to prove," she said in a determined voice.

"To Ellen?" Elizabeth asked incredulously. She didn't want Lucy to ride because of something Ellen had said!

"No, Elizabeth. To myself."

Ted gave Elizabeth a questioning look. Elizabeth shrugged helplessly. He dismounted and handed the reins and his helmet to Lucy. "Thunder's all yours," he said.

Lucy stroked Thunder's thick mane. "Come on, boy," she whispered. "I know we can do it!"

With her left foot in the stirrup, she mounted Thunder gracefully and settled gently into the saddle. There was a determined gleam in Lucy's eyes that Elizabeth had never seen before. Suddenly Lucy didn't look like the shy girl who just cleaned saddles in the tack room. She looked every bit as sure of herself as Ted did when he rode Thunder.

"Take it easy, Lucy," Elizabeth advised. *What if Lucy tries a jump she can't handle?* she wondered nervously.

"Why don't I lower the jumps a few inches?" Ted suggested.

Lucy shook her head. "Leave them just the way they are." She pressed her lips into a line and gripped the reins so tightly that her knuckles were nearly white.

With a gentle nudge of her legs, Lucy and Thunder trotted off. Lucy took him around the ring a few times, as if she wanted to get acquainted with Thunder before attempting any jumps. As they passed by, Elizabeth could hear Lucy murmuring words of encouragement to the horse. "Atta boy!" Lucy said. "Here we go, now!"

Lucy looked like a natural in the saddle, but there was an uneasy look in her eyes that made Elizabeth clench the top fence railing.

"She looks awfully nervous to me," Ellen remarked loudly as Lucy cantered by for a fourth time.

Suddenly Lucy pointed Thunder toward the first jump. Thunder cantered toward it willingly, and together they cleared the post with room to spare.

"All right!" Ted whispered.

Lucy and Thunder took the next two jumps just as handily.

"Come on, Lucy," Elizabeth murmured, crossing her fingers.

But when they approached the in-and-out, Lucy seemed to hesitate. As Thunder bore down on the double jump, Lucy's face was white with fear.

"She's chickening out," Ellen said smugly.

Almost as soon as the words were out of Ellen's mouth, Lucy and Thunder glided over the first rail. Thunder took one strong stride and sailed over the second jump effortlessly.

"Beautiful!" Ted murmured.

"Beginner's luck," Ellen muttered.

After Lucy had completed the course, Elizabeth and Ted began to applaud. "That was incredible, Lucy!" Elizabeth cried as Lucy and Thunder trotted over to them.

Elizabeth saw Lucy's hands trembling.

"Are you OK?" Elizabeth asked anxiously when Lucy had dismounted.

"Maybe you should sit down," Ted suggested.

Lucy took a deep, quivering breath. "I really did it, didn't I?" she asked, as though she couldn't quite believe it.

"You looked like a real pro out there," Ted said. "And I think Thunder enjoyed himself, too."

Lucy reached up to stroke Thunder's ear. He dipped his head and nudged her shoulder with his soft muzzle.

"I guess Lucy proved you wrong, Ellen," Ted remarked.

Ellen shrugged. "I still don't get it." She pursed her lips. "If you're such a big deal rider," she asked Lucy, "why don't you have your own horse?"

Lucy's smile faded. "I *did* have a horse," she said quietly. "A great horse."

"His name was Starfire," Elizabeth added.

"So where is Starfire now?" Ellen prodded.

"That's really none of your business, Ellen," Elizabeth pointed out, seeing the anxious look on Lucy's face.

Lucy handed Thunder's reins to Ted. "I've got to go clean some saddles. Thanks for letting me ride, Ted."

"Any time." When Lucy was safely out of earshot, Ted turned to Ellen. "You didn't have to be so nosy."

"I was just *asking*," Ellen defended herself.

"If she wanted us to know what happened to her horse, she would have told us," Elizabeth said.

But as she watched Lucy disappear into the tack room, she couldn't help but wonder what had happened to Lucy's horse.

When Elizabeth got home from the stable that evening, she peeked into Jessica's bedroom to see if she was home from the beach cleanup.

"Hi, Elizabeth!" Jessica was sitting at her desk, applying a coat of pink nail polish to her right hand. "Is that the newest look down at the stables?" she asked with a smile.

"What do you mean? I always wear these jeans."

"I meant the pieces of hay in your hair!"

Elizabeth reached up and plucked out a stray bit of hay. "Oops," she said with a laugh. "I was helping Ted and Lucy unload some fresh hay. At least the color matches my hair." She sat down on Jessica's bed. "Since when do you wear nail polish?"

"Since I started cleaning up black goop." Jessica moaned. "My hands look like Steven's after he's helped Dad work on the van."

"Well, at least it's for a good cause," Elizabeth pointed out.

"Yes," Jessica admitted. "But it's really frustrating. It seems like every time we think we're making progress, more oil appears. I'm afraid that beach will *never* be clean."

Elizabeth sat down on Jessica's bed. "By the way," she said, "how's Whiskers doing?"

"Adam called the aquarium today. Whiskers had a little bit of formula this morning, but there really hasn't been any change. He's still awfully weak. Adam and I are going back to the aquarium Saturday to visit him."

"Poor little thing," Elizabeth said sadly. "I keep remembering those big brown eyes."

"Me, too," Jessica sighed. "I'm really worried about him."

"Are you going to keep helping with the cleanup?" Elizabeth asked.

Jessica shrugged. "Adam says the weather's supposed to get bad toward the end of the week. If it rains, we won't be able to get anything accomplished. So cross your fingers."

"For what?" Elizabeth teased. "Good weather or bad?"

Jessica held up her hand and examined her nails. "Good, I guess." She smiled at Elizabeth. "And Adam kind of expects me to show up now. I'd hate to disappoint him."

Jessica was still blowing on her wet nails when she rushed to the dinner table fifteen minutes later. "Sorry I'm late," she told the family. "Nail emergency."

"Well, as long as it was something *important*." Steven groaned.

"So, how's your friend Ted doing with his training?" Mr. Wakefield asked Elizabeth as he passed a bowl of mashed potatoes to Steven.

"Great," Elizabeth said. "He and Thunder are both in top form. I'm sure they'll be able to win the competition, especially now that Lucy's helping with his training."

"Lucy? Is she your new friend at the stable?" Mrs. Wakefield asked.

Elizabeth took a bite of chicken and nodded. "Lucy's a terrific rider. You should see her jump with Thunder!"

"Why don't you invite her over sometime?" Mrs. Wakefield suggested.

Elizabeth shrugged. "OK. But I'm not sure she'd come. Lucy's a little . . . secretive. She doesn't talk much about herself. In fact, she doesn't really talk about anything except horses."

"Maybe she's just shy," Mrs. Wakefield suggested. "Or maybe she thinks you're only interested in her because she's so good with horses."

"You could be right, Mom." Elizabeth nodded thoughtfully.

"You know, you could invite your friend Adam over sometime, too," Mrs. Wakefield said, smiling at Jessica.

"No way!" Jessica scoffed. "He'd think I liked him or something. Besides—" she picked up a paper napkin, "what would he think if he saw that I'm still using *these*?"

After dinner, Elizabeth went to the phone and dialed information to get Lucy's phone number.

The phone rang twice before a deep male voice answered. "Benson residence."

"Hello. Is Lucy there?" Elizabeth asked.

"Yes, she is. This is her father. May I ask who's calling?"

"This is Elizabeth Wakefield."

"Oh, yes. Lucy's mentioned your name before. You must be one of her friends from glee club."

Elizabeth started to correct Mr. Benson, but he had already set down the phone.

A moment later Lucy picked up the receiver. "Hello?"

"Hi, Lucy. It's me, Elizabeth Wakefield."

"Oh, uh . . . hi," Lucy said quietly. "Is something wrong?"

"No." Elizabeth was surprised. Lucy sounded so uncomfortable. "I just thought I'd invite you over for dinner. Maybe tomorrow night, if you're not busy?"

"Um . . . I guess I could," Lucy said hesitantly. "I'll have to check with my parents though. Next week might be better." Lucy didn't sound enthusiastic at all.

"Well, you can let me know tomorrow," Elizabeth said. "By the way, your dad said something about glee club."

"What did you say to him?" Lucy demanded. Her voice was tense.

"Nothing. He didn't give me the chance," Elizabeth explained. "But I didn't know you were in glee club."

"I'm not!" Lucy laughed nervously. "You know how parents are—always getting things confused."

"Sure."

"Well, I have to go," Lucy said quickly. "I'll see you tomorrow. OK?"

"See you then."

Elizabeth hung up and stared at the phone for a moment. *I like Lucy,* she thought, *but I'm not sure I understand her.*

The next day at the stable, Lucy didn't mention Elizabeth's dinner invitation, and Elizabeth decided not to pursue it. For most of the afternoon, the girls timed Ted with a stopwatch as he took Thunder through his jumps.

"That's a new time record, Ted!" Lucy shouted as she clicked off the silver stopwatch.

Elizabeth glanced at the watch. "You shaved two seconds off your best time!"

Ted rode over to the fence. "You two are the best cheerleading squad a guy could ask for," he said with a laugh. "I thought maybe we'd take one last run around the course before the rain hits."

Elizabeth glanced up at the sky. Threatening gray clouds had blocked out the sun, and a chilly breeze sent the trees swaying. Sensing a storm, a frisky colt out in the pasture scampered close to his mother's side for protection.

As Ted began the series of jumps again, Elizabeth felt a cold drop of rain splatter on her arm. "He'd better hurry," she said to Lucy, as thunder grumbled off in the distance. "It's starting to look like a bad storm."

Behind them, Ellen trotted up on Snow White. "I'm going in," she said, her eyes on Ted and Thunder as they flew over a jump. "It's going to start pouring any minute now."

Snow White snorted and pawed the ground nervously. "Snow hates storms," she explained. "She gets really skittish." Ellen headed off toward the stable at a trot.

"It seems as if horses can always tell when bad weather's coming," Elizabeth said. "Even before the weatherman."

"Starfire always could," Lucy agreed. "And boy, did he hate storms!"

Just then the sky lit up with a jagged bolt of lightning. A moment later, ear-splitting thunder shook the air.

Inches before a post-and-rail, Thunder reared up on his hind legs in fear. Ted tried desperately to regain control as Thunder whinnied in terror, his big hooves flailing in the air.

The thunder was so deafening that Elizabeth could not even hear her own horrified scream as she watched Ted plunge to the ground.

Seven

◇

Ted lay motionless as big drops of rain began to splatter the ground.

"*Ted!*" Elizabeth screamed. "Are you all right?"

The only answer was a low moan.

"Hurry!" Elizabeth cried as she climbed over the fence as fast as she could. With Lucy close behind, she rushed to Ted's side and knelt beside him. His face was gray and his eyes were squeezed shut as he winced with pain. "Are you hurt?"

"It's my bad leg," Ted groaned. "I think it's broken again."

Elizabeth squeezed his hand, which was cold and clammy. "Don't worry," she said calmly. "You're going to be fine. Run and call 911," Elizabeth told Lucy. "I'll stay here with Ted. Ask Ellen or one of the stable hands to bring me a couple of saddle blankets. We need to keep Ted as warm as possible."

Lucy glanced up at the sky as the rain began to fall in heavier drops. "But the rain—" she began.

"See if you can find a poncho or an umbrella," Elizabeth said, as calmly as she could. "Hurry!"

Lucy nodded and dashed for the office.

"Why don't I just try to get up?" Ted suggested, easing up onto his elbows.

"If something's broken I don't think you should move, Ted."

"But you're going to get soaked!"

"Don't worry about *me*." Elizabeth managed a laugh.

Suddenly a blast of thunder filled the air. The rain poured down, drenching Elizabeth and Ted. Thunder trotted nervously around the ring.

Elizabeth looked up to see Ellen and two stable boys running toward the ring. Ellen was carrying an umbrella.

Ellen held the umbrella over Ted's head, making sure she stayed completely dry, too. "Does it hurt?" she asked.

"Not as much as my pride," Ted joked.

Elizabeth squeezed his arm and tried to smile. Out of the corner of her eye, she noticed Thunder cautiously approaching the group. "It's OK, boy," she called. "It's just a little rain!"

Far off in the distance, an ambulance siren howled. "Don't worry, boy," Ted said as Thunder approached him. "We're going to be fine."

After the ambulance had arrived, Elizabeth

tried to call Ted's father at the number Ted had given her. He wasn't in, but the person who answered the phone promised to give him the message. Then Elizabeth called her mother.

Mrs. Wakefield came to the stable as quickly as she could and took Lucy and Elizabeth to Sweet Valley Hospital. The girls sat in the emergency room waiting area while Mrs. Wakefield asked the receptionist about Ted's condition.

"He's in X-ray," Mrs. Wakefield told the girls when she returned. "They said it would be a while before he's ready to be released."

"Can we please wait, Mom?" Elizabeth asked. "I have to know how he's doing."

"Of course. Would you like me to see if I can reach Mr. Rogers on the phone?"

"Thanks, Mom," Elizabeth said gratefully.

While Mrs. Wakefield looked for a pay phone, Lucy and Elizabeth sat silently in the empty waiting area. Lucy seemed particularly nervous. She bounced her leg up and down, and stared straight ahead down the long corridor that led to the door labeled "Emergency."

"I hate the smell of hospitals," she muttered.

Elizabeth took a deep breath and wrinkled her nose. "I know what you mean. It does smell funny." She looked at her watch. "It's getting kind of late. Do you think you should call your parents?"

Lucy shook her head. "They're not expecting me home until six. I told them I, uh . . . would be helping Ted until late."

Mrs. Wakefield returned to the waiting area. "Ted's father is on his way. I told him we would wait until he arrives."

Suddenly Lucy reached for a magazine on the waiting room table. She held it up in front of her face and pretended to study a page intently.

"Why, hello there, Lucy!" a petite nurse in a crisp white uniform called as she passed through the waiting area. "Is that really you behind that magazine?"

Slowly, Lucy lowered the magazine. "It's me, all right," she said quietly.

"We haven't seen you lately, dear. How have you been feeling?"

Lucy's cheeks reddened. "I'm *fine*," she said emphatically.

"That's good to hear. Well, I've got to run now. Take care of yourself." The nurse continued on her way.

Lucy picked up her magazine again and stared at the page. Elizabeth noticed that her lower lip was trembling slightly.

"That nurse is—" Lucy paused for a moment, then continued, "a friend of my mom's. She lives near us."

"That's nice," Elizabeth said, exchanging a puzzled look with her mother.

"I've only met her once or twice," Lucy continued in a tight voice. "I don't know *why* she was acting so friendly!"

"I'm sure she was just trying to be nice, honey," Mrs. Wakefield said.

"Well, I wish she'd just minded her own business!" Lucy cried, her face suddenly red.

Elizabeth didn't know *what* to say. Maybe Lucy was just upset about Ted. Or maybe she just really didn't like hospitals.

At last Elizabeth decided to speak. "What's going to happen to Thunder now? There's no way Ted will be able to compete."

"Wait and see what the doctor says," Mrs. Wakefield advised. "Maybe things aren't as bad as you think."

Lucy glanced down the hall anxiously. "I'll bet Ted will be riding in no time!" she said fiercely.

"You're right, Lucy," Elizabeth agreed. "Maybe it was just a sprain." She desperately wanted to believe her own words, but she knew it was unlikely Ted would ride again soon. His leg had already been badly hurt once. It would probably take even longer to heal this time.

The doors to the emergency room opened and an orderly appeared, pushing a wheelchair. In it sat Ted. His left leg was extended out in front of him, and a sheet was draped over it.

"Ted!" Elizabeth cried.

"He's a little fuzzy," the orderly advised. "Painkillers."

"I feel great!" Ted said with a goofy smile. He leaned toward Elizabeth. "Just tell me one thing, Elizabeth."

"What, Ted?"

"How am I going to ride Thunder with *this*

on my leg?'' He pulled back the sheet to reveal a brand-new plaster cast that extended all the way up to his knee.

Ted insisted on showing up at the stable that Saturday, crutches and all. He put on a brave face, asking all the riding students to sign his cast, and joking about being the first one-legged blue ribbon champion in Sweet Valley's history. But Elizabeth could see the disappointment in his eyes as he watched Ellen practice her jumps.

"When will the cast come off, Ted?'' Lucy asked.

"Six weeks, at least,'' Ted answered. "Maybe longer.'' Suddenly he pounded the fence with his fist. "I might as well face it. I'm going to have to sell Thunder.''

"But you can't!'' Elizabeth cried. "There's got to be another way!''

"Maybe Mr. Carson will give you another extension,'' Lucy suggested.

"He's already given me three,'' Ted reminded her. "And besides, where would I come up with the money, even if he *did* give me more time? I've run out of options.''

"It's just not fair,'' Lucy moaned. "Thunder's such a great horse, and you've practiced so hard.''

"When I think of all the help you and Elizabeth gave me . . .'' Ted's voice trailed off. "What a waste.''

Suddenly Elizabeth had a wonderful idea. "It doesn't have to be a waste, Ted!''

"What are you talking about?"

"I know someone who knows the course practically as well as you do," Elizabeth said. "And Thunder is comfortable with this rider." She gazed at Lucy and smiled encouragingly.

A smile dawned on Ted's face. "It's perfect!" he cried. "*Lucy* could ride Thunder in the competition!"

Lucy's mouth dropped open. "*Me?*" she asked in amazement.

"You're a great rider, Lucy!" Elizabeth said encouragingly. "You could enter in the hunters class, and you'd have a real chance of winning the prize money."

Lucy shook her head so furiously that her black curls went flying. "No way!" she said. "You two have lost your minds!"

Elizabeth and Ted looked at each other. "I've still got my mind," Elizabeth said seriously. "How about you, Ted?"

"As far as I know, mine's still in working order," Ted answered with a grin. "How about it, Lucy? It's my only chance. And Thunder's."

Lucy looked from Elizabeth to Ted and back again. "I can't," Lucy said, her voice nearly cracking. "I'd like to help you keep Thunder, Ted, but there's no way I could do what you're asking."

"Do what?" Ellen asked, riding up on Snow White.

"We're trying to talk Lucy into competing on Thunder in my place," Ted explained.

"But I *can't*," Lucy repeated sadly.

"You mean you *won't*," Ellen said. "I knew

you were all talk, Lucy Benson! It's easy to show off when there's no pressure. But you're afraid you'd fail in a real competition, aren't you?"

Lucy stuck out her chin. "That's not it at all, Ellen!"

"It doesn't matter," Elizabeth told Lucy in a soothing voice. "We understand." But Elizabeth wasn't quite sure she *did* understand. Couldn't Lucy see that she was Ted's only hope?

"I'm really sorry, Ted," Lucy almost whispered.

Ted shrugged. "Don't worry about it, Lucy. I understand." Ted looked away. "I think I'll go spend some time with Thunder. I'm sure he's wondering why we're not riding today."

Ted trudged away slowly on his crutches, his head bowed. Elizabeth's eyes burned with tears as she watched him go.

You might as well get used to it, she told herself. *Soon Thunder will be gone forever.*

Eight

◇

"I'm glad you're on the other side of that glass," Jessica muttered as she peered into the huge fish tank in the main exhibition room at the aquarium. A tiger shark glided slowly past, revealing a mouthful of razor-sharp teeth.

"He's a mean-looking guy, isn't he?" Adam asked.

Jessica nodded. She gazed at a fish with brilliant yellow and blue stripes. "Now *this* is what the ocean is supposed to look like."

"Not covered with oil and filled with garbage," Adam agreed. "Whiskers would like it here."

"Let's go see him," Jessica said excitedly.

Adam led the way to the animal infirmary where Whiskers spent most of his time. "Well, look who's here, Whiskers," said Dr. Robinson when Adam and Jessica entered. "It's your rescuers!"

"Hi, there," Jessica said, poking a finger through Whiskers' cage door.

Whiskers edged forward clumsily on his little flippers. *"Krooh!"* he said, making the same sad sound Jessica had heard the first time she'd seen him on the beach.

Jessica turned to Dr. Robinson. "Poor guy, all locked up in there. Can't you let him out for a swim?"

"I'm afraid not, Jessica," the doctor said kindly. "We're worried that the poisons in Whiskers' system may cause his breathing to shut down, so we want to have him as close as possible to our emergency equipment."

Whiskers touched Jessica's finger with his cold, wet nose.

"But he looks so miserable," Jessica protested.

"I imagine he feels pretty miserable," Dr. Robinson replied. "He's not out of the woods yet."

"You don't mean he's going to . . ." Jessica trailed off, afraid to say the word.

"We've taken care of a lot of seals like Whiskers here," Dr. Robinson added. "It's much too early to give up hope, Jessica." He looked at his watch. "It's just about time to give him his fish milk shake. Do you feel like playing seal mother for a while? Whiskers definitely seems to like you."

"Sure!" Jessica said enthusiastically. "I'd love to. In fact, I'll come every day after school to help feed him until he's all better."

"I think Whiskers will be very pleased to hear that," Dr. Robinson said. "Wait here, and I'll go get his formula."

Dr. Robinson returned, carrying a baby bottle filled with the thick, brownish liquid. He started to hand the bottle to Jessica, then paused. "You know, Whiskers hasn't really learned table manners yet," he said. "I'm afraid he'll ruin your nice outfit."

Jessica glanced down at her brand-new pair of khaki shorts.

"Who cares?" she said, reaching for the bottle of formula. "I've got a hungry seal to feed!"

"I just don't know why Lucy won't help you out, Ted," Elizabeth said the next day as she measured oats into a bucket. "It doesn't make sense."

Ted leaned his crutches against the wall of the feed room and sat down on a bale of hay. "There's no point in pressuring her, Elizabeth," he said in a resigned voice.

"I'm not going to. But I *know* she could win that competition. You said yourself that Ellen Riteman has a good chance at winning, and Lucy is a much better rider than Ellen."

Ted put his finger to his lips and nodded toward the door. "Hi guys," Ellen said. "How's the leg, Ted?"

"Great," Ted said with a grim smile. "I'll be running marathons in a day or two."

"Tough break," Ellen remarked. "Break—get it?" Ellen laughed heartily at her own joke. "Mr Carson told me you got the list of competition entrants in the mail yesterday."

Ted reached into his shirt pocket and pulled out a typewritten list. "Here," he said. "You can take a look if you want. I was just going to post it on the bulletin board in the office."

Ellen reached for the paper eagerly. "Let's see," she murmured. "Sally Owen, George Bullock . . . Well, *they're* no threat to me. Colleen Stanley—her quarter horse always refuses at least one jump . . ." She continued scanning the list while Elizabeth and Ted exchanged a look of amusement.

"Hi, everybody," Lucy said quietly, stepping into the feed room. "Are you still talking to me?"

"Of *course*," Elizabeth assured her. "Don't be silly!"

"I really feel like I'm letting you down," Lucy said apologetically.

"Hey, it's not your job to rescue me," Ted said. "Don't worry about it, Lucy."

"But I would if I could, Ted—" Lucy began.

"*Sure* you would," Ellen interrupted. She waved the list of entrants in the air. "I recognize most of these people, and I know I can beat all of them," she told Ted confidently. "Of course, there's a few people I've never heard of." She glanced at the list again. "Mary Beck, Anita Vasquez, Alison Thatcher . . . Ever heard of any of them?"

"Let me see that list!" Lucy demanded.

Ellen shrugged and handed her the paper.

"Alison Thatcher," Lucy repeated, staring intently at the list.

"Is she a friend of yours, Lucy?" Elizabeth asked.

Lucy smiled. "Not exactly."

Ellen snatched back the list. "I don't know why you care who's entering, anyway," she said with a superior smile. "It's not as if you're going to ride."

Lucy crossed her arms over her chest. "That's where you're wrong, Ellen."

"Lucy!" Elizabeth cried in amazement. "You mean you're going to enter the competition?"

Lucy nodded, and Ellen's smile suddenly faded.

"But why?" Ted asked.

"Yes, *why*?" Ellen echoed nervously.

Lucy nodded toward the list in Ellen's hand. "Let's just say I still have something to prove."

When Jessica had finished feeding Whiskers, she and Adam headed for the beach to help with the cleanup effort.

"Look at all the volunteers," Jessica said as she and Adam pedaled their bikes into the parking lot.

"I'll bet there are a hundred people!" Adam cried.

"Hurry, Adam," Jessica said impatiently as he locked his bike to the bike rack. "I can't wait to get started."

"You *can't*?" Adam laughed. "I was starting to get the idea you were sick and tired of the cleanup."

Jessica felt her cheeks begin to warm. Was it that obvious? "I guess I *was* getting a little tired of going home every afternoon covered in oil. And I was getting pretty frustrated," she admitted. "But after spending the morning with Whiskers, I feel good about it again." The cleanup had long ago ceased to be just an excuse to see Adam. Jessica knew that by cleaning the beach she was also helping Whiskers.

"You've really grown attached to him, haven't you?" Adam asked as they began trudging across the sand.

Jessica nodded. "Before Whiskers, I never even liked animals very much. He's the closest I've ever come to having a pet."

"He really likes *you*. I couldn't believe it this morning when he fell asleep in your lap after you fed him!" Adam stopped walking and touched Jessica's shoulder. "But you shouldn't think of him as a pet, Jessica. Don't get too attached, OK?"

Jessica's stomach tightened into a painful knot. "You mean . . . because he might die?"

"Well, it is possible," Adam said gently. "And even if Whiskers *does* live, you have to remember he's a wild animal. It's not good for him to get too attached to humans. Someday, Whiskers will have to survive on his own again."

Jessica didn't want to think about losing Whiskers right now. It was just too painful. Maybe Adam was wrong. Maybe she and Whiskers could stay friends somehow. It was possible, wasn't it?

Just ahead of them, a group of high school students was shoveling dirty sand into a large wheelbarrow. "The beach is actually starting to look better," Jessica said optimistically.

Adam pointed toward the rocks where Jessica had found Whiskers. "Those big rocks are almost back to normal."

"Jessica! Jessica Wakefield!" Jessica turned and saw Ellen Riteman running toward her across the sand.

"Jessica!" Ellen called, panting. "Wait up!"

"Hi, Ellen," Jessica said. "Did you come to volunteer?"

"Are you crazy?" Ellen looked at Adam and gave him a big smile.

Jessica sighed. "Ellen, this is Adam. Adam, meet Ellen."

"Hi," Adam said. "Nice to meet you."

"Jessica, I have to talk to you," Ellen said urgently. "In private. Unicorn business."

Jessica rolled her eyes. She had a funny feeling that whatever was bothering Ellen wouldn't be nearly as important as Jessica's own worries.

"I'm going to go say hi to some of the other volunteers," Adam said, smiling.

"You'll never guess what happened!" Ellen said as soon as Adam was gone.

"What?" Jessica asked, crossing her arms over her chest.

"Well, you know Ted Rogers broke his leg."

"Elizabeth told me about it," Jessica said.

"Well, I just found out that Lucy Benson is going to ride his horse Thunder in the competition!"

"So?"

"So? *So?*" Ellen cried. "So we'll be competing in the same event! What if she beats me? Thunder's a very good horse, Jessica."

"You're always saying it's the rider and not the horse who wins the competition," Jessica pointed out. "Is Lucy a better rider than you?"

"She *thinks* she is." Ellen kicked at a shell with her foot. "But she's all talk. Besides, I think there's something very strange about that girl."

"Strange how?" Jessica asked.

"Strange, like she won't tell anyone where she learned about horses. And she claims she owned a horse, but she won't say what happened to him. I think she has a secret she doesn't want anyone to find out." Ellen glanced over her shoulder. "That's why I came here to see you."

Jessica narrowed her eyes. "I don't get it, Ellen. This is *not* Unicorn business. And if you have a horse question, you should be asking Elizabeth."

"That's just the point! Elizabeth and Lucy are friends. I want you to find out everything you can about Lucy. Elizabeth must talk about her."

"I haven't seen much of Elizabeth lately," Jessica admitted. "I've been here at the beach practically every day."

"Well, nose around," Ellen urged. "Keep your eyes open. I want to know what it is Lucy is hiding."

"But *why?*"

"Because I've worked way too hard to let her steal *my* blue ribbon away," Ellen replied determinedly. "If Lucy Benson has some kind of secret, then I'm going to find out *exactly* what it is!"

Nine

"I'm so glad you finally decided to come over to my house for dinner," Elizabeth said on Thursday afternoon as she and Lucy walked home from the stables. "It'll give us a chance to get to know each other better. It seems like all you, Ted, and I have been able to talk about all week is the competition."

"That's all I can *think* about, anyway." Lucy laughed.

"Me, too," Elizabeth agreed. "I'm so excited, I almost feel like *I'm* the one who's going to be competing."

"Sometimes I wish it *were* you instead of me," Lucy admitted. "I'm so afraid I might let Ted down. Or worse."

"Worse? What do you mean?"

Lucy shrugged. "Oh, nothing," she said

quickly. "You know—falling on my rear end and looking like a fool. Something like that."

"I wouldn't worry too much about *that*. Ted says he's positive you're going to win."

"I don't know. There are going to be a lot of good riders at the competition," Lucy said seriously. "*Really* good riders."

"Like that girl on the entrants list?" Elizabeth asked.

"Alison Thatcher." Lucy spoke the name as if it hurt her to say it.

"Is she a very good rider?"

Lucy nodded. "Yes. And she's got the ribbons to prove it."

The girls turned the corner onto the Wakefields' street. "Well, *you* have ribbons, too," Elizabeth reminded Lucy. "And on Saturday, you'll have another one!"

Lucy turned to Elizabeth and smiled gratefully. "Thanks, Elizabeth. It's nice to have you rooting for me."

"By the way," Elizabeth continued, "I've been thinking about doing an article on the regionals for our sixth-grade newspaper. Sort of a behind-the-scenes look at the competition. I was hoping you would let me do an interview with you."

"But I *couldn't*!" Lucy exclaimed.

Elizabeth laughed. "Don't worry. It would just be a few simple questions about how you prepare for a competition."

"No, I mean it, Elizabeth," Lucy insisted. "I really don't want to be interviewed."

"Why not?" Elizabeth asked, feeling frustrated.

"I'm just . . . I don't know . . . too shy."

"That's OK, Lucy," Elizabeth said slowly. "Maybe I'll interview Ellen instead. After all, she *is* a sixth-grader."

"That's a good idea." Lucy looked very relieved.

When they reached the Wakefields' house, Elizabeth introduced Lucy to Mr. and Mrs. Wakefield and then took her upstairs. They found Jessica in the bathroom, scrubbing her nails with a nail brush. Two large streaks of oil decorated her cheeks, and the floor of the bathroom was covered with a dusting of black sand.

"Jess, this is Lucy Benson," Elizabeth said.

"Lucy, the horse girl?" Jessica asked with interest, peering over her shoulder.

Lucy laughed. "That's me!"

"It's nice to finally meet you, Lucy," Jessica said enthusiastically. "Elizabeth's told me *so* much about you!"

Elizabeth stared at her twin in surprise. She had hardly seen Jessica lately, and she was almost positive she'd only mentioned Lucy once or twice. Something was definitely up.

"I'm sorry about the mess in here," Jessica apologized.

"Jessica's been working on the beach cleanup," Elizabeth explained.

"How's it going?" Lucy asked.

"Not bad." Jessica rinsed her hands under the faucet. "The coordinator of the cleanup says we're actually ahead of schedule." She washed off her face and dried it on a towel. "But enough about me. I want to hear all about you and Thunder!"

Elizabeth narrowed her eyes. Since when did Jessica ever get tired of talking about herself?

"Are you feeling OK, Jess?" Elizabeth inquired politely.

"Of course," Jessica answered lightly. She turned her attention to Lucy. "Come on, Lucy. I'll show you my room."

Elizabeth and Lucy followed Jessica into her room and sat on the bed.

"I wonder where I put my copy of *Black Beauty*?" Jessica muttered as she searched her desk.

"*Your* copy?" Elizabeth repeated in amazement.

"Oh, I loved that book!" Lucy exclaimed.

"Me, too," Elizabeth agreed. "I've read it three times."

"So tell me all about yourself, Lucy. When did you start riding?" Jessica inquired sweetly.

"Oh, a while ago," Lucy answered vaguely.

"Do you have your own horse?"

Lucy shifted uncomfortably. "Not anymore."

"What happened to him?" Jessica pressed.

"Jessica!" Elizabeth scolded. "It's really none of your business."

"Do you know what time it is, Elizabeth?"

Lucy asked suddenly, peering around the room for a clock.

Elizabeth checked her watch. "It's ten after six, Lucy. Why?"

"No reason." She reached for her book bag and climbed off the bed. "I'll be back in a second," she said, heading for the bathroom. "I'm just going to take an aspirin."

"Do you have a headache?" Elizabeth asked.

Lucy nodded. "Just a little one."

"There's some aspirin in the medicine cabinet," Elizabeth said.

"That's OK. I've got some in my book bag."

As Lucy entered the bathroom, Elizabeth noticed her pull a medicine bottle out of her bag. Lucy glanced up, and quickly closed the door.

"That didn't look like an aspirin bottle," Jessica whispered.

"It's really none of your business," Elizabeth pointed out, although she was thinking the same thing herself. "And while we're at it, since when are you so interested in my riding friends?"

"I've always been interested in them," Jessica responded in a wounded voice.

"Name one!"

Jessica grinned. "How about Ted Rogers? I was interested in him."

"You know what I'm talking about. Jess," Elizabeth hissed.

The bathroom door opened and Lucy stepped back into Jessica's room.

"Why don't we go downstairs now?" Elizabeth suggested. She didn't want Lucy to be subjected to any more of Jessica's prying questions. "It's almost dinnertime."

"Wait until you taste my mom's lasagna!" Jessica said, jumping off the bed. "It's incredible!"

"Good," Lucy said with a smile. "Because I'm *starving*!"

Just as they reached the stairs, the phone rang. "I'll get it," Jessica said, rushing back to the telephone in the upstairs hallway.

Elizabeth and Lucy were in the kitchen helping Mrs. Wakefield make a salad when Jessica came downstairs several minutes later. Her face was splotchy and her eyes were red. She slumped down in a chair at the kitchen table without saying a word.

"Honey, what's wrong?" Mrs. Wakefield asked worriedly.

"That was Dr. Robinson," Jessica murmured. "I made him promise to call me if there was any change in Whiskers' condition." Tears welled up in her eyes. "He says Whiskers may be dying."

"Honey, I'm so sorry!" Mrs. Wakefield gave Jessica a comforting hug.

"Whiskers is a seal Jessica's been helping to care for at the Sweet Valley Aquarium," Elizabeth explained to Lucy.

"What's wrong with him?" Lucy asked.

"Something I can't pronounce," Jessica said miserably. "He's been poisoned by the oil spill." She rubbed her eyes. "I just fed him this afternoon! He didn't eat very much, but he seemed OK."

"You can't give up on him, Jess," Elizabeth said. "You said yourself Whiskers has a lot of spunk. I'm sure he'll be fine."

"That's not what Dr. Robinson told me," Jessica responded glumly. "He said I shouldn't get my hopes up." She stood up slowly and headed toward the hallway. "Do you mind if I skip dinner, Mom? I'm just not hungry anymore." Without another word, Jessica disappeared.

Jessica hardly slept that night. First thing in the morning, she called the aquarium to check on Whiskers' condition. She was told that he wasn't scheduled for surgery until ten that morning. The veterinarians would attempt to clear a blockage in Whiskers' lungs.

At school, Jessica tried to concentrate on all the things she usually found so important, but her mind kept drifting to images of Whiskers. She could see his big, dark eyes and hear his sad, little bark. After sitting restlessly through her second period science class Jessica knew what she had to do.

As soon as the bell rang, she leaped from her seat and rushed into the hallway.

"Jessica, what is the *matter* with you? Why are you in such a hurry?" Lila demanded when she finally caught up with her. "You've been acting strange all morning. When I made that funny joke about Lois Waller during homeroom, you didn't even laugh."

"There are more important things in this world than making fun of people, Lila," Jessica snapped.

"Like what, exactly?"

"Like life and death!" Jessica cried.

"Who died?" Lila asked casually.

"No one, yet," Jessica answered quietly. "But Whiskers is really sick."

"Oh, is *that* all?" Lila said with a smirk. "I thought you were serious."

"I *am* serious," Jessica whispered. "That's why I'm on my way to the nurse's office. I'm going to pretend to be sick so I can get out of school."

"You're skipping school and you didn't even invite me?" Lila sounded hurt.

Jessica sighed. Lila was definitely starting to get on her nerves. "I'm skipping school so that I can visit Whiskers."

Lila glanced at her watch. "Well, when you're done with that seal, you'll still have plenty of time to go to the mall, right? Maybe I should skip with you."

"I'm really not in the mood for the mall, Lila."

"But *I* am," Lila insisted. "I haven't bought any new clothes in *ages*."

Jessica tried to ignore the twinge of envy she felt. She had more important things to think about than the fact that Lila was spoiled rotten. "There's the nurse's office," she said. "How do I look?"

"You look awfully healthy to me."

"I thought I'd pull the old thermometer on the light bulb trick. It's not as gross as pretending to throw up."

"Well if you're pretending to have a fever, you should pinch your cheeks to make them look flushed," Lila suggested helpfully.

"Good idea!" Jessica stopped in the middle of the hallway and pinched her cheeks a few times. Then, for good measure, she slapped them lightly.

"How's that?" Jessica asked.

"Better." Lila nodded. "I have to get to class. I've already been late twice this week. Good luck!"

Jessica stopped in front of the office labeled "School Nurse." Outside the frosted glass door, she pinched her cheeks again. Then, hanging her head in her best imitation of a sick person, Jessica went inside.

"And who have we here?" Nurse Higgins asked. Her white uniform was perfectly starched and her black hair was tied into a neat little bun.

Jessica slowly approached her desk. "Um, Jessica Wakefield," she said in a weak voice. "I'm not feeling very well."

"Uh-huh. What's the matter?"

"I have a fever . . . I mean, I *think* I have a fever," Jessica answered. "It's probably just a twenty-four hour flu or something. I'm sure I'd feel better if I could just go home and rest in bed."

"Are you sure you don't have Friday Disease?"

Jessica looked puzzled. "Friday Disease?"

"That's the mysterious ailment a student gets when it's almost the weekend and the weather's especially nice."

"I'm sure it isn't that." Jessica attempted a little cough for added effect.

Nurse Higgins narrowed her eyes. "Follow me, then." She got up from her desk and led Jessica to the next room. Jessica sat down quietly on the cot. She was relieved to see a bright lamp on the wall just over her head.

Nurse Higgins pulled a white curtain around the cot. She removed a thermometer from a glass beaker filled with alcohol, wiped it dry, and placed it under Jessica's tongue. "I'll be back to check it in just a few minutes."

As soon as Nurse Higgins was gone, Jessica pulled the thermometer from her mouth and reached up to the lamp. Carefully, she touched the end of the thermometer to the hot light bulb.

Just then she heard Nurse Higgins' office door open.

"Hello."

"Why, hello there, Lucy," Nurse Higgins replied. "I haven't seen you around here lately."

Lucy! Jessica thought. *Could it be Lucy Benson?*

"Well, I haven't forgotten my pills lately," Lucy said with a laugh. "Until today, that is. I don't know what I could have done with them. I must have left them at home."

"Don't worry," Nurse Higgins replied. "That's

why your doctor arranged for me to keep a prescription here for you."

Jessica heard the sound of a cabinet opening, followed by water running into a glass. "Here you go, Lucy," Nurse Higgins said.

"Thanks."

"So how have things been going for you?" Nurse Higgins asked. "Have you been able to make new friends here in Sweet Valley? I know it must have been hard for you, having to leave your old school."

"Actually, I'm kind of used to it. My dad gets transferred a lot in his job. He's the best man in his company," Lucy said proudly, "and they're always sending him to a new office to get things organized. But he says he thinks we'll be in Sweet Valley for a long time."

"That's nice. You sound like you're proud of your dad."

"I am," Lucy said softly. "But . . ."

"But what?"

"Oh, nothing. It's just . . . it's just that ever since we found out about my problem, he's been treating me like a baby!"

Jessica strained to hear what would come next.

"Your parents are worried about you," Nurse Higgins said. "That's only natural."

"I know, but they made me sell my horse! And they haven't let me ride since I had the accident."

"Yes, I remember your parents saying something about that when they enrolled you. But don't you think they're just looking out for you?"

"They *think* they are," Lucy explained, "but my doctor said that it's perfectly safe for me to ride, as long as I stay on my medication and wear a helmet."

"Give your parents some time, Lucy," Nurse Higgins advised. "They'll come around."

"But I don't *have* much time!"

"What do you mean, dear?"

For a second, there was silence. Then Lucy spoke. "Never mind. Anyway, thanks for talking to me, Nurse Higgins."

Jessica listened as Lucy closed the office door behind her. For this amazing bit of detective work, Ellen Riteman would owe Jessica for a long time to come!

Ten

◇

Suddenly, Jessica remembered the thermometer in her hand. She touched the thermometer to the light again, and popped it back into her mouth just as Nurse Higgins returned.

"How are we doing?" she asked Jessica as she reached for the thermometer and held it up to the light. "Hmm," she murmured. "You must be *very* sick."

"I told you," Jessica said triumphantly. Then, remembering she was supposed to be suffering, she managed a little coughing fit. "I guess I'll just *have* to go home. Although I hate to miss school."

Nurse Higgins shook her head. "I'm afraid there's no doubt about it, Jessica. You've got Hamburger Syndrome for sure."

"Hamburger Syndrome?"

"It's very rare," Nurse Higgins explained. "Fortunately for all of us, it's not contagious."

Jessica frowned. Was it possible she really *was* sick? She felt her forehead. Come to think of it, it *did* feel a little warm.

"What exactly *is* Hamburger Syndrome, anyway?" Jessica asked nervously.

"It's when you run a temperature that's as high as a well-done hamburger!" Nurse Higgins held the thermometer close enough for Jessica to read it. "Really, Jessica," she said in an amused voice. "One hundred and seven degrees? That's overdoing it just a little, don't you think?"

"Boy, I must be *really* sick!" Jessica replied sheepishly.

"It's a miracle your hair hasn't caught fire yet." Nurse Higgins pointed toward the door with her thumb. "Back to class, pronto."

"All right," Jessica said meekly, shuffling toward the door.

I tried, Whiskers, she thought as she walked down the hallway.

"The library's awfully full for lunchtime," Elizabeth whispered to Amy as they sat down at a table.

"It's because they're serving mystery meat in the cafeteria!" Amy said, laughing. "I guess we're not the only ones who decided to pass it up."

"I'm excited about doing the research for my article," Elizabeth continued.

"I think the riding competition will make a great story," Amy whispered.

"I thought I'd check to see if anyone from Sweet Valley Middle School has ever won any big riding competitions. Ted Rogers is the only person I know of, and he's in high school now. I'm going to look in the back issues of newspapers."

"Wow! That's going to be a lot of work, Elizabeth. It'll take you the whole lunch period, at least."

Elizabeth shrugged. "It's either that or mystery meat!"

After checking in the Reader's Guide to Periodical Literature, Elizabeth went over to the long shelf on which old newspapers and other periodicals were kept. It took her ten minutes to collect all the papers she was looking for.

Most of the articles weren't very useful. But near the end of the lunch hour, Elizabeth discovered a large news item about the Grove Hills Invitational Horse Show. "Grove Hills," she murmured. "That's where Lucy lived before moving to Sweet Valley."

"Did you find something interesting?" Amy whispered.

"I don't know yet," Elizabeth said as she scanned the piece.

The article continued on to another page of the newspaper. Elizabeth turned the page and gasped.

The article was illustrated with a large photograph of a magnificent horse sailing cleanly over a jump. But the horse's rider was flying backward through the air, her face frozen in a look of absolute terror.

The rider was Lucy Benson!

According to the story, Lucy had fallen from her horse, Starfire, on the final jump. There was no apparent reason for the fall. Lucy had been taken away in an ambulance, and Alison Thatcher had gone on to win the blue ribbon.

So this is what Lucy's been hiding! Elizabeth thought. She felt a little bad for having discovered Lucy's secret. After all, if Lucy didn't want anyone to know what had happened to her, then it was none of Elizabeth's business. Still, people often fell off horses. Why would Lucy be so embarrassed about it?

"Amy," Elizabeth whispered. "Suppose someone doesn't want you to know about something, but you find out about it accidentally. Should you still pretend not to know?"

"Is it something important?" Amy asked.

"It could be."

Amy chewed on her pencil. "Well," she said at last, "as long as you found out totally by accident, it seems like it would be dishonest to go on pretending you didn't know."

"Thanks, Amy," Elizabeth said, folding up the newspaper. "I guess I need to have a talk with Lucy."

*   *   *

During lunch, Jessica ran to the pay phone in the lobby to call the aquarium. Her fingers trembled as she dialed the number.

"Could I speak with Dr. Robinson?" Jessica asked as soon as the receptionist at the aquarium picked up the phone.

"May I ask who is calling?"

"Jessica. Jessica Wakefield. It's very important that I get hold of him."

A moment later, Dr. Robinson came on the line. "Jessica? I was going to call you this afternoon."

"I couldn't wait until then," Jessica explained. "How is Whiskers doing? Did the surgery go OK?"

"I'm afraid I don't have a lot to report yet. Whiskers made it through surgery, but the next forty-eight hours will be critical."

"What does that *mean*?" Jessica pressed. "If he made it through surgery, doesn't that mean he'll live?"

"I'm sorry, Jessica. It's not quite that easy. But with you pulling for him, Whiskers stands a good chance."

"Can I come see him this afternoon?"

"He's sedated right now, Jessica. He'll probably sleep for the next day or two. Why don't you call me again tomorrow and I'll let you know how he's doing?" Dr. Robinson suggested. His voice was so gentle and kind that Jessica suddenly felt like crying.

"Jessica? Are you OK?"

"I'm fine," Jessica lied. "I'll talk to you tomorrow, Doctor."

Jessica walked slowly to the cafeteria and slumped down into a chair at the Unicorner.

"What are *you* doing here?" Lila exclaimed. "Didn't Nurse Higgins fall for the old thermometer trick?"

Jessica shook her head.

"Too bad," Lila said. "You could have missed mystery meat day." She poked at her lunch with a fork. "Honestly, I can't understand why they don't just let us send out for pizza!"

"Is something wrong, Jessica?" Ellen asked. "You seem sort of sad."

"She's all upset about her pet seal," Lila explained, winking at Ellen.

"Lila," Jessica growled, "if you don't shut your mouth this instant I'm going to dump that mystery meat in your lap. Worse yet, I'll make you *eat* it!"

Suddenly Jessica remembered what she'd overheard in the nurse's office. "Oh, Ellen," she said. "I heard something today about Lucy Benson that you might find very interesting."

"What?" Ellen cried, nearly dropping the carton of milk she was holding.

"Well, I was in Nurse Higgins' office . . ." Jessica began.

"What has that got to do with Lucy?" Ellen demanded.

"Just relax, Ellen," Jessica said. "I'm getting to that."

"OK, OK," Ellen replied. "I'm relaxed."

"While I was sitting there behind the curtain trying to fake a temperature, I heard Lucy come in," Jessica said. "I could hear everything she said to Nurse Higgins."

"And?" Ellen pressed.

"And, for one thing, she takes some kind of prescription medicine."

"So what?" Lila interrupted. "I have a cousin with diabetes, and he has to take medicine every day."

"I also heard that Lucy's parents don't want her to ride anymore. Lucy had some sort of accident," Jessica replied.

Ellen sat back in her chair, a look of triumph in her eyes. "So *that's* why she's always so secretive," she said. "I'll bet her parents don't even know she's planning on riding Ted's horse in the competition."

"I guess that means after Lucy beats you Saturday, she'll get grounded," Lila joked.

"If Lucy's parents find out tomorrow before the competition, she won't even be there!" Ellen cried, ignoring Lila's remark. "That way she won't have the chance to steal my blue ribbon!"

"What are you going to do?" Jessica asked.

Ellen snorted. "What do you *think* I'm going to do? I'm going to call Lucy's parents and tell them!"

"Do you know the number?" Lila asked.

"No, but I'm sure I can find it," Ellen replied.

"How many Bensons can there be in Sweet Valley?"

"This seems like an awful lot of trouble over a stupid contest with a bunch of jumping horses," Lila commented. "First it's Jessica and her dumb seal. Now it's you and your dumb horse!"

"Since when do you call a thousand dollars dumb?" Ellen responded.

"Did you say a *thousand* dollars?" Lila's eyes widened.

Ellen nodded. "That's what I'll get if I win. I expect all my fellow Unicorns to be there tomorrow to cheer me on. Because I'm sure I'll want to spend part of my prize money on a big party for all my truly *loyal* friends."

"I can't make it," Jessica stated. "I've got to help Adam and see about Whiskers."

"Consider it an official Unicorn meeting," Lila reminded Jessica. "You *have* to be there. Besides, Ellen needs our support." She grinned widely at Ellen. "Now, just exactly what kind of party were you planning on, anyway?"

By the time Elizabeth arrived at the stables on Friday afternoon, Lucy was already there. Elizabeth found her in Thunder's stall, carefully plaiting his mane in preparation for the competition.

"Elizabeth!" Lucy said. "You're just in time to help me with these braids. They take forever!"

"Too bad Jessica isn't here," Elizabeth laughed. "She's great with hair."

Lucy handed Elizabeth a mane comb and a spool of thread. "Hold these, will you?"

Elizabeth watched as Lucy began carefully plaiting a new section of Thunder's mane. "You're going to look so handsome, Thunder," Elizabeth murmured in his ear.

Thunder snorted.

Elizabeth turned her gaze back to Lucy. "So how do you feel about the competition tomorrow, Lucy? Are you nervous?"

"*That's* the understatement of the year." Lucy looked up from her braiding and met Elizabeth's eyes. "I hardly slept at all last night. I'm so afraid I'll let you and Ted down."

"Just do the best you can, Lucy."

"It's been such a long time since I've competed. What if I . . ." Lucy's voice trailed off.

"Lucy, I don't mean to pry," Elizabeth began. She hoped she was doing the right thing.

"What is it?"

"I was doing some research in the library today for the *Sixers* article I told you about. I came across something in the *Grove Hills Chronicle*—"

"Then you know," Lucy interrupted, keeping her eyes on Thunder's mane.

"Is that why you've been so secretive?" Elizabeth asked gently. "Because you fell once? But *everybody* falls sooner or later. It's no big deal if you're a good rider and you've been taught how to fall so you won't get hurt."

"I *am* a good rider and I *do* know how to fall," Lucy said.

"Then what's the problem? One fall isn't the end of the world."

"Elizabeth," Lucy said, lowering her voice. "That wasn't just an ordinary fall."

"Why?" Elizabeth asked softly.

Lucy took a deep breath. "The reason I fell off Starfire that day," she said slowly, "is because I have epilepsy."

Eleven

◇

"I didn't know about it until that day at the competition," Lucy continued. "Right in the middle of the course I began to have this strange, mixed-up feeling in my head. The next thing I knew, I was in an ambulance on my way to the hospital."

"You must have been scared," Elizabeth said sympathetically.

"You bet I was! I was afraid I was going crazy or something. Then the doctors did an EEG—that measures the electrical activity of the brain—and a bunch of other tests. And that's when they discovered I had epilepsy."

"I guess I really don't know very much about epilepsy, Lucy."

"You're not alone." Lucy smiled. "I didn't, either. But it's really pretty simple. A seizure happens when there's a sudden change in the way brain cells send electrical signals to each other. The rest of the time, the brain works just fine. It's really not so scary once you understand what's happening."

Lucy continued to plait Thunder's mane. "The good thing is, there are medicines you can take to help prevent seizures."

"Is that the medicine you took when you came over to dinner the other night?" Elizabeth asked.

Lucy nodded.

"Why didn't you just tell me you have epilepsy?" Elizabeth asked. "It's not as though it would make a difference in our friendship."

"Maybe it wouldn't make a difference to *you*, Elizabeth," Lucy replied bitterly. "But it does to some people."

"But why, Lucy?"

Lucy concentrated on the braid she was making. After a few seconds, she spoke. "You should have seen my friends at the stable after my accident. As soon as they found out I had epilepsy, they wouldn't come near me. To tell you the truth, Elizabeth, I was relieved when my dad told me we were moving to Sweet Valley. It meant I'd have the chance to make a fresh start."

"Don't any of your other friends know about this?"

"Just a couple," Lucy replied. "And now you."

"How did they take it when you told them?"

Lucy looked up. "They were pretty understanding about it, actually. But I can't count on everyone to be that way." She sighed. "My own parents aren't handling it very well."

"What do you mean?"

"My doctor says that as long as I take my medicine, I can lead a completely normal life. My epilepsy isn't very severe and it's thoroughly under control. But my parents just can't seem to believe it's true. As soon as they found out, they sold Starfire. And then they told me I could never ride again, even though my doctor says it's perfectly OK as long as I stay on my medication and wear a helmet."

"So your parents have no idea that you've entered this competition?" Elizabeth asked.

Lucy shook her head. "It's the only way, Elizabeth. Don't you see? I have to prove to my parents once and for all that they need to treat me like a normal person."

"But don't you feel guilty, keeping the truth from them?"

"I feel *terrible*," Lucy admitted. "But I'll feel much worse if I can't ever go back to leading a normal life. You've got to help me keep my secret, Elizabeth. Tomorrow, after the competition, I'll tell my parents. But in the meantime, I'm trusting you to help me."

Elizabeth took a deep breath. "All right, Lucy," she agreed at last. "If your doctor says it's OK for you to ride, and you're sure you want to go through with the competition, then I'm on your side."

Thunder nickered softly and bobbed his head.

"And so is Thunder," Elizabeth added with a laugh.

Later that afternoon, Elizabeth found Jessica sitting in the den, staring at a blank TV screen. "Is something wrong, Jess?"

Jessica didn't answer.

"Jessica!" Elizabeth called. "Did you hear me?"

"What?" Jessica shook her head and glanced up. "Oh, hi, Elizabeth. Where have you been?"

"At the stable." Elizabeth sat down next to Jessica on the couch. "Any word on Whiskers?"

Jessica shook her head. "He made it through the operation, but Dr. Robinson says we won't know much before tomorrow."

Elizabeth put her arm around her twin. "I really hope he'll be OK, Jess. I know how much you care about him."

"Adam says I care too much," Jessica said gloomily. "He's afraid I don't understand that because Whiskers is a wild animal, he'll have to go back to the ocean one day."

"It's hard *not* to get attached, though," Elizabeth said.

"All I want is for Whiskers to get better! Right now I'd give anything just to see him swimming in the ocean with his seal friends!"

"He's going to be fine, Jess. Just wait and see." Elizabeth nodded toward the blank TV screen. "By the way, were you watching something on TV?"

"No. I'm saving electricity. Too many people leave the TV on even when there's nothing they really want to watch. And there wasn't anything I wanted to watch so I turned it off."

"But you were staring at it when I came in."

Jessica shrugged. "I was depressed. I always watch TV when I'm depressed."

Just then the phone rang. "Would you get it, Elizabeth?" Jessica asked.

Elizabeth picked up the receiver. "Wakefield residence. Um, just a second, Ellen. I'll see."

Jessica rolled her eyes. "Oh, all right," she said reluctantly.

Elizabeth handed Jessica the phone. "Hi, Ellen. Could we make this quick, please? I'm really not in the mood to talk."

For a few minutes Jessica listened impatiently. "I don't know what to tell you, Ellen. Just keep trying." She sighed deeply. "Are you sure you have the right Bensons?"

Elizabeth gave Jessica a questioning look. Suddenly feeling uncomfortable, Jessica lowered her voice. "Look, Ellen," she said quickly. "I've got to go. This isn't a very good time, if you know what I mean."

"What did Ellen want?" Elizabeth asked suspiciously when Jessica had hung up the phone.

"Oh, nothing. Nothing you'd be interested in, anyway."

"If it has to do with Lucy Benson, I'd be very interested," Elizabeth said firmly.

"It's Unicorn business," Jessica replied. "I wouldn't want to bore you with it." She stood and headed toward the kitchen. "I have to set the table," she called over her shoulder.

"I'll help." Elizabeth jumped up to follow Jessica. If Ellen Riteman was up to something involving Lucy, she was determined to find out what it was!

Elizabeth pulled five plates out of the cupboard. "You know," she said casually, "I thought you *liked* Ted Rogers."

"I do like Ted Rogers," Jessica replied as she grabbed a handful of forks.

"Well, if Lucy doesn't win that competition tomorrow, Ted is going to lose Thunder."

Jessica winced. Her reaction told Elizabeth all she needed to know. Ellen was *definitely* up to something. "Ellen wouldn't be planning to pull some underhanded trick, would she, Jess?"

"How would *I* know?"

"Jessica," Elizabeth insisted, "this is *really* important!"

"Oh, all right! I have more serious things to worry about right now than whether or not Ellen gets her stupid blue ribbon!" Jessica cried. "Ellen found out that Lucy's parents don't want her to ride. She's going to call the Bensons and tell them Lucy's going to be in the competition tomorrow."

"How could Ellen be so sneaky?" Elizabeth demanded angrily.

"Well, from the sound of it, your friend Lucy's being pretty sneaky herself."

"That's different," Elizabeth said softly. *Lucy has a good reason*, she added to herself. "Ellen hasn't gotten hold of the Bensons yet, has she?"

"I guess not. No one answers at the number she's been calling."

Elizabeth put down the plates she was holding and went straight to the telephone.

"What are you going to do?" Jessica asked.

"I'm going to call Lucy and warn her!" Elizabeth said.

But there was no answer at the Benson residence. "*Now* what am I going to do?" Elizabeth asked Jessica when she hung up. "It's too late for me to ride over to Lucy's house—even if I knew where she lives!"

Jessica shrugged. "Look on the bright side, Elizabeth. If you can't get hold of Lucy, then neither can Ellen."

Elizabeth groaned. Somehow, Jessica's reasoning wasn't exactly reassuring.

"Elizabeth! I thought you'd gone to bed. Who are you calling at this hour of the night?" Mrs. Wakefield asked as she paused in the upstairs hallway. "It's nearly eleven-thirty."

Elizabeth put down the receiver. She'd been calling the Bensons all night long and had still gotten no answer. "Lucy Benson," she told her mother.

"To wish her luck? Lucy is probably in bed by now. And that's where you should be, too."

"I know, Mom."

"What time does the competition start?"

"It starts at ten, but Lucy and I are going to meet Ted at the stable earlier so we can help him get Thunder ready for the trailer."

"How do you think Lucy will do tomorrow?" Mrs. Wakefield asked.

"I think she's got a good shot at winning," Elizabeth answered hopefully. *Unless Ellen ruins everything,* she added silently.

Elizabeth said good-night to her mother and crawled into her bed. *Ellen's probably given up trying to call the Bensons by now,* she told herself. *With any luck at all, Lucy could still pull it off.*

Twelve

◇

"Lucy, where have you *been*?" Elizabeth demanded, dashing into the stable early Saturday morning.

"What do you mean?" Lucy asked, as she attached a stable bandage to one of Thunder's legs. The bandage would protect him during the trip to the competition grounds.

"Did anyone call your house last night?" Elizabeth asked.

Lucy shook her head. "I wouldn't know. We were having dinner at my grandparents' house. We didn't get home until late. Why?"

Elizabeth leaned against the wall of Thunder's stall and let out a sigh of relief. "Thank goodness!"

"Elizabeth, what's going on?"

"Ellen found out that your parents don't want you to ride. She was planning to call your parents and tell them about the competition so you wouldn't be able to ride today and she'd have a better chance at winning. As soon as Jessica told me about the plan yesterday evening, I tried to call you."

"Am I glad we were at my grandparents' house!" Lucy exclaimed. Her face darkened. "But what if Ellen calls this morning before our event?"

"My guess is that she'll be too preoccupied to try anything this late," Elizabeth said. "Try not to worry about it, Lucy. You've got more important things to think about."

"Hey, champ! Are you ready for your big moment?" Ted called as he came into the stable.

"As ready as I'll ever be," Lucy said.

"You and Thunder are in top form," Ted encouraged her. "Nothing's going to stand in the way of that blue ribbon now!"

"I hope you're right, Ted." Lucy looked at Elizabeth and crossed her fingers.

"I had no idea how big this place was!" Elizabeth exclaimed as Ted's father pulled to a stop in the crowded, grassy field of the state fairgrounds. Around them were hundreds of other cars and trucks, each with a covered horse trailer in tow.

"It's the biggest show in the state, after the Delmar National," Ted said. "There will be hundreds of horses and riders competing in all kinds of events. Steeplechase, dressage, you name it. The junior hunter event is only a small part of it."

"Maybe so," Elizabeth said as she climbed out of Mr. Rogers' truck and stretched her legs, "but look at those stands! I'll bet there are a thousand people there already." Elizabeth saw Lucy gazing intently at the bleachers. "Don't worry, Lucy," she whispered. "Even if your parents *were* up there, you'd never be able to spot them."

"I know. But I'm just so worried that they'll show up and ruin everything."

Elizabeth was beginning to wish she hadn't told Lucy about Ellen. Lucy was already jittery. But it hadn't seemed fair not to at least warn her about Ellen's plan.

"You're right, Elizabeth," Lucy said, shielding her eyes from the bright morning sun. "I have something *else* to worry about. And there she is."

Elizabeth followed the direction of Lucy's gaze. A tall, slender girl with a honey-colored braid down her back was leading a beautiful black quarter horse. "Is that Alison Thatcher?" Elizabeth asked.

Lucy nodded. "Yes. And her horse Black Magic. We've competed against each other three times. The first time, she beat me. The second time, I beat her. The third time . . . I fell."

"Are you ready to unload Thunder?" Ted called.

The girls ran to the back of the trailer. "Thunder's going to be a bit cramped after the ride over," Lucy said. "I'm glad we'll have some time to get him loosened up."

Ted watched while Elizabeth untied Thunder and Lucy pulled down the small trailer ramp. "I wish I could be more help," Ted apologized. "But these crutches kind of get in the way."

"That's OK, Ted," Elizabeth smiled. "We need you here for moral support."

"I guess I'll be heading over to the stands," Mr. Rogers said as he came around to the back of the trailer. "You three seem to have things under control."

"Thanks, Dad," Ted said. "We'll meet you after Lucy accepts her blue ribbon!"

"Good luck, Lucy," Mr. Rogers called.

"With Thunder *and* Lucy, we won't need much luck," Ted said confidently.

"Good luck, all the same." Mr. Rogers gave Ted a pat on the back and headed toward the bleachers.

Lucy and Elizabeth carefully led Thunder out of his trailer. As soon as the horse reached the bottom of the ramp, he flared his nostrils and whinnied loudly.

Ted laughed. "That's right, boy. Let everybody know that Thunder has arrived!"

The girls carefully removed the stable bandages from Thunder's legs. While Lucy positioned his saddle and secured the girth, Elizabeth and Ted checked him over carefully.

Lucy returned to the truck and retrieved a blue riding jacket and her helmet. "I had it in my book bag, so it's a little wrinkled," she said as she pulled on the jacket.

"You look wonderful!" Elizabeth exclaimed.

"Perfect," Ted agreed.

Together the group walked Thunder past rows of horse trailers. As they approached the ring where the hunter event was going to take place, Lucy paused to watch the workers busily checking the post-and-rails. Near the ring, competitors paced their horses back and forth. Others practiced their jumps in the large field close by.

"I don't see Ellen anywhere," Ted remarked. "You don't suppose she decided not to show up, do you?"

Elizabeth glanced nervously at Lucy, but Lucy didn't seem to have heard Ted's question.

"I'll be right back," Lucy said. She led Thunder over to where Alison Thatcher was inspecting one of Black Magic's hooves.

"Hello, Alison," Lucy said quietly.

Alison glanced up in surprise. "Lucy! What a surprise! I didn't expect to see *you* here."

Lucy smiled. "I'm full of surprises."

Alison glanced up at Thunder. "So I see. New horse?"

"He belongs to my friend Ted. His name is Thunder."

"He's a beauty." Alison grinned slyly. "In fact, I'd say he's probably the *second* best horse here today."

"We'll see about that," Lucy said with a laugh. "See you later."

Lucy returned to Ted and Elizabeth. "Alison thinks she's going to beat me. It's too bad I'm going to have to disappoint her!"

"That's the spirit!" Ted grinned.

Lucy looked up at Thunder. "What do you think, boy?" she asked. "Can we beat them?"

Thunder threw up his head and whinnied loudly.

"I'd say that was a definite *yes!*" Lucy mounted Thunder. "We're going to go warm up a bit." For a moment she glanced up at the spectator stands and scanned the rows anxiously. Then she trotted off toward the field.

Ted and Elizabeth sat down on a soft patch of grass near the ring. They were looking over the other competitors when Ted suddenly nudged Elizabeth. "There's Ellen."

Ellen, with most of the Unicorns by her side, was leading Snow White. Elizabeth saw her twin in the middle of the group. Jessica's face was creased with a frown, and she didn't seem at all interested in the talk going on around her.

When Ellen saw Ted and Elizabeth, her jaw dropped open in surprise. "Ted! Elizabeth! What are you doing here?"

"What do you think we're doing here?" Elizabeth asked.

"Did you come to cheer me on?" Ellen smiled nervously.

"Actually, they came to cheer *me* on."

Ellen whirled around. "*Lucy!*"

"Yes, Ellen. I'm *still* here," Lucy said angrily.

"Of . . . of course you are. Why wouldn't you be?" Ellen shot a suspicious glance at Jessica.

"I can't think of any reason," Lucy said. "Unless, of course, some sneak had tried to keep me from competing today. Sorry, Ellen, but it looks like your little plan failed."

Ellen's face flushed and her eyes blazed angrily. "I wouldn't be too sure about that, Lucy." Ellen stomped off, yanking at Snow White to follow.

"It wouldn't have done you any good, anyway," Lucy called after her. "Either way, Alison Thatcher would have beaten you. But since I'm here, the best you can hope for is third place!"

Lucy dismounted. In spite of her brave words, Elizabeth could tell she'd been very upset by Ellen's last remark.

"You don't think she got through to my parents this morning, do you, Elizabeth?" Lucy asked, her face pale.

"I doubt it," Elizabeth reassured her.

"Would somebody please tell me what's going on around here?" Ted interrupted. "I'm totally confused."

"We all are, Ted," Lucy replied with a faint smile.

"While you explain everything to Ted, I'm going to catch up with Jessica." Elizabeth dashed off after the Unicorns. "Jessica!"

Jessica turned around and waved. She broke off from the Unicorns and walked back to Elizabeth.

"Was Ellen mad at you?" Elizabeth asked.

Jessica shrugged. "It's hard to tell."

"Do you know if she got hold of Lucy's parents this morning?"

"She hasn't said anything to me. I don't think

Ellen likes me very much at the moment. She wasn't very happy with the way I cut her off on the phone last night. But, she's sure been pretty confident this morning."

"That's not a good sign," Elizabeth said anxiously. "By the way, how's Whiskers doing? Any more news?"

"No change," Jessica replied glumly. "I called the aquarium first thing this morning."

Jessica looked over her shoulder at Ellen and the rest of the Unicorns. She lowered her voice. "I have to cheer for Ellen because of the Unicorn loyalty and all, but tell Ted good luck."

"I will," Elizabeth promised.

She ran back to Ted and Lucy. Ted was slowly shaking his head back and forth and looking at Lucy with admiration. "I can't believe you've been keeping all this a secret, Lucy. Are you sure you want to go through with the competition?"

"Absolutely," Lucy assured him.

"Jessica says good luck," Elizabeth said as she joined them.

Ted nodded toward the ring. "It's time to get ready. The first horse is about to start."

They watched as a boy on an Appaloosa entered the ring. A horn sounded, signaling that he had sixty seconds to begin the course. There were eight jumps carefully arranged in the large ring.

The boy cleared the first and second jumps with no problem. But as his horse turned sharply toward the third jump, Ted shook his head. "His stride's too long," he murmured.

Sure enough, the Appaloosa's next jump was too low, and he knocked the rail down. He went on to make the next three jumps, but missed the last two.

Two more horses followed, and each missed one of the jumps. Ted turned to Lucy. "It's that third jump that's getting everyone."

Lucy nodded. "I'll have to be careful to get Thunder positioned just right coming off the second post-and-rail."

"Is that Alison Thatcher up next?" Ted asked.

"That's her, all right," Lucy replied.

Black Magic sailed over the first two jumps as if he were flying. He took the troublesome third jump with ease, and finished the rest of the course perfectly.

"She *can* ride," Ted admitted. "But you're better, Lucy."

"Thanks, Ted. We're up. I'd better get in position," Lucy said.

"Good luck, Lucy." Elizabeth stroked Thunder's neck. "You too, boy."

"Go get 'em, Thunder!" Ted cried.

As Lucy rode off, Elizabeth looked nervously at Ted. "Keep your fingers crossed."

Ted tapped his fingers nervously on his crutches. "All she has to do is hit one fence," he said, "and I lose Thunder."

"She won't, Ted." But in her heart, Elizabeth

wasn't so confident. Lucy had her parents to worry about, as well as Alison Thatcher!

Lucy and Thunder entered the ring and awaited the starting horn. Thunder stood perfectly still, his chestnut coat glistening in the bright sunshine. Elizabeth and Ted made their way through the crowd gathered next to the ring so they could get a better view.

The horn sounded and Lucy and Thunder cantered into position. Thunder glided easily over the first jump.

"That's one down!" Out of the corner of her eye, Elizabeth saw a couple pushing their way through the crowd. She turned her attention back to the ring, just in time to see Lucy and Thunder clear the second jump with room to spare.

"Beautiful!" Ted said.

"*There* she is!" a woman cried.

Elizabeth jerked around to see the middle-aged woman wave her arm in the air. "Lucy!" the woman called.

"Oh no," Elizabeth moaned.

Lucy saw her parents just as Thunder came into position for the treacherous third jump.

Thirteen

◇

"She'll miss the jump!" Ted cried.

Thunder seemed to sense that Lucy's concentration had been broken. His position was off by a wide margin as his powerful legs coiled to jump.

As the big horse rose from the ground, Elizabeth's heart seemed to stop. Thunder's front legs cleared the fence, but as he sailed over the rail, his rear hooves clipped the top.

As the rail wobbled and bounced dangerously, Elizabeth grabbed Ted's hand. "Please stay up," she whispered.

The rail settled back into place.

"They made it!" Elizabeth cried, breathing a sigh of relief. She turned back to see Lucy's parents. They were holding onto each other, their faces filled with fear.

Quickly, Lucy regained control of Thunder, and they took the remaining jumps effortlessly.

"She did it!" Ted said, grinning from ear to ear. "There's still the next round for the entrants who didn't knock down any jumps, but at least she made it this far."

"I'm not so sure there's going to be a jump-off for Lucy," Elizabeth said, nodding toward Mr. and Mrs. Benson.

They watched as Lucy rode over to her parents. "We'd better go talk to them," Ted said. "It's my fault Lucy's riding to begin with."

As soon as Lucy had dismounted and stepped out of the ring, Mrs. Benson rushed over to her and gave her a long hug. "Honey," she cried, "we were so frightened for you! As soon as we got the phone call from your friend Ellen, we rushed over."

"She's not my friend, Mom." Lucy's face was flushed with the exertion of riding.

"You shouldn't have disobeyed us like this, Lucy," Mr. Benson said sternly.

"I'm afraid it's my fault Lucy's riding today, sir," Ted said, stepping forward awkwardly on his crutches. "I'm Ted Rogers, the owner of the horse Lucy is riding. When I injured my leg, Lucy offered to ride Thunder in the competition so I could use the prize money to pay for his upkeep."

"You acted very irresponsibly, young man," Mr. Benson said angrily. "How could you let someone with Lucy's condition—"

"He didn't *know* about my epilepsy, Dad," Lucy interrupted. "It's not Ted's fault."

Mr. Benson's expression softened. "I know

how much riding means to you, Lucy. But your mother and I care so much about you. We don't want you to take unnecessary risks."

Just then Alison Thatcher walked by, leading Black Magic. "Nice ride, Lucy," she called.

Lucy waved. "Do you remember her?" she asked her parents. "That's Alison Thatcher. Last year she and I were even in the Grove Hills competition. Then I had my seizure and fell, and Alison won." Lucy's eyes welled up with tears. "Just because I know I have epilepsy now doesn't mean I'm going to let Alison win today! I'll have epilepsy all my life, and I can't always let everyone win, just because I'm afraid to compete, or because my parents are afraid to let me compete." Lucy took a deep breath. "If Alison beats me, well, that's OK. She's a good rider. But if you make me stop now, it won't be Alison who beat me, it'll be my epilepsy that beat me!"

For a few moments no one spoke. Then Mrs. Benson put her arm around Lucy. "If you're brave enough to ride again, I think your father and I should learn to overcome our own fears," she said softly. "We can't offer you any guarantees, Lucy. But since the doctors say it's OK for you to ride, maybe we should let you do the thing you love." She looked over at Mr. Benson. "Still, you shouldn't have disobeyed us. It's up to your father to decide whether or not you can continue the competition today."

Everyone looked at Mr. Benson expectantly.

Elizabeth held her breath as Lucy turned to her father. "Well, Dad?" she asked softly.

"There's just one thing I want to know, Lucy,"

"What's that?" Lucy asked anxiously.

"Where are we going to put all the trophies you'll be bringing home?"

There were a total of five riders in the final jump-off to determine the winner in the junior hunters competition—Lucy, Alison, Ellen, and two boys. Riders would be judged on speed, as well as on making all jumps cleanly.

One of the boys was first. He moved too quickly through the jumps, and missed the final post-and-rail.

"That's one down," Lucy muttered.

The second boy was more cautious. His horse cleared all of the fences, but his final time—ninety-two point five seconds—was not a very good one for the course.

"So it's just the three of us," Ellen said, glancing nervously at Lucy and Alison, who both ignored her. Ellen waved to the Unicorns, who were bunched together at the far end of the ring, by the third jump. They waved back enthusiastically.

Ellen moved Snow White into position and adjusted her helmet. As the horn blew and Ellen readied herself to start, the Unicorns lined up along the fence just as if they were at a Boosters practice, ready to practice cheers.

Lucy saw Ellen shaking her head back and forth and glaring at her friends. "They wouldn't be *that* dumb, would they?" Lucy whispered to Alison.

With an anxious expression on her face, Ellen spurred Snow White on. They cleared the first fence and the second. Then, just as Ellen tried to set Snow White up for the difficult third post-and-rail, the Unicorns let out a huge cheer.

"Y-A-A-A-Y, ELLEN!" they cried in unison.

Snow White whinnied in surprise and balked at the jump, planting her hooves firmly on the ground. Ellen tried desperately to hold on, but Snow White had stopped too suddenly. Ellen flew into the air and sailed cleanly over the fence— without her horse!

The crowd was silent as Ellen got to her feet. But once it was clear that she wasn't hurt, the crowd broke out in laughter. Ellen picked up her riding crop and rushed toward the Unicorns, swinging it wildly. The girls ran off in all directions, screaming.

Lucy turned to Alison Thatcher. "Just the two of us, Alison."

"Just like old times," Alison said with a smile.

Lucy watched anxiously as Alison and Black Magic prepared to start the course. At the sound of the horn, they took off at a lightening-quick pace, flying over the first two jumps with ease.

At the third jump Alison reined in Black Magic expertly before urging him back into a breathtakingly fast canter. He was a black blur as he sailed over the third fence and raced down the course.

Lucy watched in admiration as her rival flew over the remaining jumps. Her final time was an amazing eighty-eight point seven seconds.

Lucy took a deep breath. Her heart was pounding wildly and her mouth was dry. Suddenly she had a terrible thought. *What if I get so tense that I have a seizure?* she wondered frantically. She looked over at Ted and Elizabeth and her parents. So many people were counting on her to succeed! What if she let them down?

Beneath her, Thunder shifted nervously. Lucy realized that he was sensing her mood. If she was tense about the course, Thunder would be, too.

Lucy bent low over Thunder's head and put her mouth close to the horse's ear. "All right, boy," she whispered. "There are a lot of people counting on us. Are you ready?"

Thunder snorted and pawed at the ground.

"OK, then. If you can do it, so can I!"

Lucy walked Thunder to their starting position. At the sound of the horn, she signaled him and he cantered swiftly to the first jump.

Lucy tightened her legs against Thunder's flank, urging him forward. She felt the power of the huge animal rising up beneath her. The sound of his pounding hooves stopped, as rider and horse soared together through the air.

Lucy and Thunder seemed to hang in the air for a moment before pounding back down to earth. Thunder readied himself for the second post-and-rail and they were over it in a flash.

Lucy knew that the next jump would determine the outcome of the competition. Alison had taken just a split second to orient Black Magic for the jump. If Lucy was going to beat her time, she would have to go straight into the jump at nearly full speed.

"It's up to you, Thunder!" she whispered. She felt him ready for the leap, and the next thing she knew they were flying through the air like a pair of birds.

Thunder took the rest of the course effortlessly. As they came to the finish, Lucy glanced quickly at her mom and dad. It was hard to tell who was cheering louder—her parents, or Elizabeth and Ted!

Lucy reined Thunder in and patted his neck. "Thank you, boy," she whispered.

A hush fell over the crowd as they waited to hear the announcement of Lucy's time.

At last the announcer spoke. "That's a new course record, folks. Eighty-six point five seconds for Lucy Benson, on her horse, Thunder!"

"I think this belongs to you, Ted." Lucy walked over to Ted and handed him the thousand-dollar check she'd just received from the judges.

"How can I ever thank you, Lucy?" Ted asked. "I'd like you to have part of the money. After all, you did all the work!"

"Don't forget Thunder," Lucy said with a laugh, reaching over to stroke Thunder's muzzle. "Anyway, I've got what I came for." She held up her blue ribbon for everyone to see.

"We're so proud of you, honey," Mrs. Benson said.

"I knew you could do it, Lucy," Elizabeth added happily.

"Nice job, Lucy."

Lucy turned to see Alison Thatcher. "You too, Alison," she said.

"I'm sure we'll meet again," Alison said. "Only next time, *I'll* be taking home the blue ribbon."

"Don't count on it," Lucy said with a laugh.

"By the way," Alison said, "I heard a rumor that Starfire might be up for sale. Seems his new owner thinks he's too spirited."

Lucy looked at her parents hopefully.

"You know," Mr. Benson said, smiling. "I *do* kind of miss that old bag of bones."

Lucy gave her father a long hug. Then she turned to Elizabeth. "Where's your notebook?" she asked.

"What do you mean?" Elizabeth asked.

"You told me that you wanted to interview the winner of the competition for the *Sixers*!"

"I thought you wanted to keep things a secret."

"Not anymore," Lucy answered. "I've had enough secrets for a lifetime!"

*   *   *

"Who won the competition?" Jessica asked.

"Don't you know?" Elizabeth was surprised.

"I missed the ending. Ellen chased us halfway across the fairgrounds before she ran out of steam."

Elizabeth giggled. "Lucy won."

"I'm glad," Jessica said as she headed for the front door.

"Where are you going, Jess?"

Jessica grinned. "To the aquarium, of course. It's time for Whiskers' afternoon feeding."

"But I thought—"

"Dr. Robinson called me a few minutes ago. Whiskers woke up and drank two whole bottles of his formula. And he wants more!"

"Jessica, that's wonderful!" Elizabeth cried, giving her twin a joyful hug.

"Dr. Robinson said if he keeps eating like that, Whiskers can go back to his home in a few weeks." Jessica reached for the door.

"Wait a minute, Jess," Elizabeth said. "Can I go with you?"

"Sure," Jessica said happily. "And now that you're through helping Lucy and Ted with the competition, you'll probably want to put in some time at the beach cleanup."

"That would be great," Elizabeth said. "I'd really like to help out."

"I've got an entire wardrobe of oily clothes for you to choose from," Jessica said with a laugh.

Fourteen

◇

"All right. All together, now. Heave!" Dr. Robinson shouted, as he and Adam and two workers from the Sweet Valley Aquarium each lifted a corner of the canvas sling from the back of the pick-up truck. Inside the canvas, Whiskers squirmed nervously.

During the month that Whiskers had spent at the aquarium, he had grown to be as big as a large dog—and he was ten times as slippery.

"Hang in there, Whiskers," Jessica called, standing beside him. "Just a few more minutes and you'll be free."

Dr. Robinson had parked the truck on the beach, right beside the rocks where Jessica had first found Whiskers. A camera crew from the local TV station had come to document Whiskers' release.

Jessica smiled. It was wonderful to have the beach back the way it had been before the oil spill. But there was one thing left to do. Jessica had known all along that Whiskers would have to go back to the sea, but in her heart she'd hoped this day would never come.

Almost every day she'd visited Whiskers at the aquarium. She had helped Dr. Robinson as he taught Whiskers how to eat whole fish instead of fish milk shakes. And later, she had assisted when it was time to teach Whiskers how to catch live fish.

Then one day Dr. Robinson explained that he thought the time was right to release Whiskers back into his natural home.

Now, as Dr. Robinson, Adam, and the other two men lifted Whiskers again and began to carry him down toward the water's edge, Jessica felt tears coming to her eyes.

"Don't worry, Jessica," Elizabeth said, putting her arm around her twin's shoulder. "He'll be all right."

"I know *he'll* be all right," Jessica said. "But what about me? I'll probably never see Whiskers again!"

"You can't be sure, Jessica. Seals have always lived near these rocks. There are some out there now. One of them might even be Whiskers' mother!" She gave Jessica a reassuring smile.

"Maybe Whiskers will stay around this area. Now that we've cleaned it up, it's a pretty nice neighborhood."

The group had reached the water's edge and Jessica trudged down to join them. She could see Whiskers' eyes gazing out to sea.

"Can you see the other seals out there, Whiskers?" Jessica asked. "They all want to be your friends." She swallowed the lump in her throat. "That's where you belong, boy. Out in the nice, clean ocean."

Dr. Robinson and Adam stepped into the gently lapping surf and carefully lowered Whiskers into the water. The seal slipped from the canvas sling into the ocean. But instead of moving directly out to sea, the seal turned and looked back at Jessica with his huge, dark eyes.

"No, you can't stay with me," Jessica replied, her voice cracking. "You have to go, Whiskers!"

Slowly Whiskers turned away and swam into the surf. Jessica watched as he dove under the water and disappeared from sight. A few minutes later she saw his gray head poking up out of the water. The other seals gathered around him like a welcoming committee.

A large wave washed over them, and when it had passed, Whiskers and the other seals were gone.

"Good-bye, Whiskers," Jessica whispered. "Good luck!"

"Are you going to be OK?" Elizabeth asked.

"Of course," Jessica said, wiping away a tear.

"You know me, Elizabeth. I don't even *like* animals!"

What will be Jessica's next surprising new interest? Find out in Sweet Valley Twins No. 46, **MADEMOISELLE JESSICA.**

Created by Francine Pascal

Jessica and Elizabeth Wakefield have had lots of adventures in *Sweet Valley High* and *Sweet Valley Twins* . . .

Now read about the twins at age seven! All the fun that comes with being seven is part of *Sweet Valley Kids*. Read them all!

THE SADDLE CLUB

Bonnie Bryant

Share the thrills and spills of three girls drawn together by their special love of horses in this adventurous series.

First love . . . first kiss!

A terrific series that focuses firmly on that most important moment in any girl's life – falling in love for the very
first time ever.

Available from wherever Bantam paperbacks are sold!